Suddenly, Sapphire's clothes seemed to jump back at her.

"Wh-*at*?"

A girl in a black jumpsuit leapt out of the wardrobe, brandishing what looked a lot like a knife. She began to swing the weapon around. Kerri screamed. The four members of the group backed against the walls of their cramped dressing room.

"There's no need for this," Fox said, trying to take command. "Come on, *calm down*. What's wrong?"

The girl was about fourteen, wore too much make-up, and had mad eyes.

"Where's Trudi Garth?" she demanded. "Where is she?"

"She's not arrived yet," Fox told her. "The Ghosts aren't on till last."

A vein rose up on the girl's forehead and began to quiver. She was still holding the weapon, which Sapphire saw was a screwdriver. Its shaft looked awfully sharp.

POINT CRIME

DYING FOR YOU

David Belbin

SCHOLASTIC

For Mike Atkinson

Scholastic Children's Books
Commonwealth House, 1–19 New Oxford Street,
London WC1A 1NU, UK
a division of Scholastic Ltd
London ~ New York ~ Toronto ~ Sydney ~ Auckland
Mexico City ~ New Delhi ~ Hong Kong

First published in the UK by Scholastic Ltd, 1999

Copyright © David Belbin, 1999

ISBN 0 590 54292 3

Typeset by TW Typesetting, Midsomer Norton, Somerset
Printed by Cox & Wyman Ltd, Reading, Berks.

10 9 8 7 6 5 4 3 2 1

Prologue

Security at the arena was tight. Lianne kept her head down so that she wouldn't be recognizable on any surveillance videos. She broke away from the gaggle of girls by the stage door. Lianne had made herself up to look much older than she was, but so had all the other girls. She wouldn't get away with pretending to be one of the road crew's girlfriends. So she made her way to the main entrance instead.

A neon sign above the doors announced *The Smash Hits* "New Millennium Tour". Tonight's show featured the biggest boy and girl bands of the year. Lianne wanted to get as close to them as she could. If she got close enough, one particular star was going to remember her for ever.

The concert didn't start for over an hour. They'd only just started letting the audience in. Lianne joined the queue. Once inside, she headed not for the seats, but for some toilets at the far corner of the hall. The NEC Arena was one of those places where they changed the layout according to what kind of show was on – everything was movable, not just the seating.

Lianne opened a door marked *No Entry*. The area she found herself in had a very temporary feel to it. There was no security in sight. A flimsy hardboard partition created a narrow walkway. What was behind it?

Still no security guard and no video surveillance camera to be seen. Lianne took the screwdriver from her purse and went to work on one of the hardboard sections. There were only six screws holding it together. The first one came away easily. So did the second. Then the third. And the fourth.

"Hey!"

Lianne slipped the screwdriver inside her jumpsuit and turned around to face the security guard.

"You shouldn't be in here. What do you think you're doing?"

Lianne glanced at the partition. The missing screws weren't obvious. She made her right arm tremble.

"Can't you tell?" she said plaintively. "I'm having some kind of seizure. I was looking for First Aid."

The security man looked sceptical for a moment, but Lianne managed to make her face go pale. She was a good actress.

"You'd better come with me," he said.

"I'm not meant to be moved when I'm like this,"

Lianne said. The last thing she wanted was to be put in some medical section where they'd call her parents and she'd miss the show. She made her whole body shake.

"Wait right there," the security man said. "I'm getting a doctor."

Once he was out of sight, Lianne whipped out the screwdriver, crouched on the ground, and undid the bottom screw. Now the partition was held together by the top screw, which was out of reach. It didn't matter. Lianne managed to push the boards apart and slipped through. The boards twanged back together as the security man returned.

"She was here, I swear," the guard said. "Where did she go?"

"We'd better check the toilets," said a female voice, presumably a doctor. "Did she tell you what was wrong with her?"

"Just that it was a seizure."

"Epilepsy?"

"She didn't say."

"Some of these girls get hysterical at the idea of seeing a real pop star."

Lianne heard the footsteps moving away and breathed a sigh of relief. She got out her lipstick and made a mark on the partition, a small heart shape which would enable her to identify the escape route later. Then she hurried down the narrow corridor.

When she got to the end of the temporary partition, Lianne could see the big revolving stage, which allowed one band to set up while the other was still playing. She'd read all about it in a magazine. But where were the dressing rooms?

There were plenty of people around. Lianne had to make her move quickly before one of them clocked her. She crouched by the side of a speaker stack. The bands wouldn't be here yet. They'd have done their soundcheck before the fans were let in. Now they'd be having a meal or a drink back at their hotels. The girls waiting at the backstage-door might get a glimpse of them as they arrived. But Lianne wanted to get closer than that.

Then she saw what she was looking for, far away at the other side of the stage. The dressing rooms were in a neat line. No names on the front, only numbers. *BAND 1*, *BAND 2* and so on. No need to guess who the number one band was. Lianne looked around. There wasn't anybody within fifty metres of her. Now was as good a time as any. She charged out of her hiding place and over to the dressing room, where she opened the door and slipped inside.

As expected, they weren't there. Nobody was. Lianne waited a moment for the door to open again, but no one came. She hadn't been spotted. Lianne didn't dare turn on the light, but her eyes soon became accustomed to the darkness. There was a big, walk-in wardrobe right opposite her. Lianne stepped into it. She felt her way to the back, then waited patiently, all the time holding her sharpened screwdriver hard against her heart.

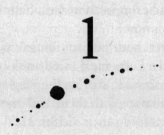

1

"What kind of dressing room's this?" Sapphire asked, flinging open the door to room number one, then closing it again. "You're never putting all four of us in there!"

"You were expecting a room each, maybe?" Hud, their manager, asked.

"One for the boys and one for the girls would be appropriate," Kerri pointed out. "Just for modesty."

"No room for modesty in this game," Hud told them. "Go on, get in there. You're on first."

As if they were likely to forget. Kerri stuck her tongue out at the manager. Hud was balding, thirty-something, and a one-time member of a group called Famous, who had had two hits while Sapphire was still at primary school. But he was in charge, so Sapphire admired Kerri's cheek.

This was their big chance of success. Nine months ago, at the auditions, the four of them had seen off a hundred other singers and musicians who wanted places in the group. Hud had made it clear that, if any of the chosen four didn't come up to scratch, they'd be out in an instant. Sapphire wasn't going to blow it now.

The manager had put his entire savings into creating Face To Face. He'd hired session musicians and a top producer. He'd brought in big-name songwriters to collaborate with them, and one of the best TV ad directors to do their videos. He'd started his own label, CPM, to ensure that he and the group kept most of their earnings. Then he'd done a licensing deal with a major label to ensure that their music was distributed properly. Finally, he'd rented the four of them a big house in Barking, where they'd been living, writing and rehearsing for months. Tonight was the moment of truth.

The dressing room had just one shower and there was only enough room for two people to sit in front of the mirror.

"Ladies first," Art said, and Kerri took one of the stools in front of the mirror.

"You go ahead of me," Sapphire told Art. "Age before beauty."

Art laughed. At nineteen, he was the oldest member of the band. Art was tall to the point of gawkiness. His face had an angular quality. It could be made to look good in photos. In real life, however, his looks were uninspiring, even a little geeky. It didn't matter. For Art had a gorgeous voice: George Michael meets Michael Jackson. He sang lead on their first single, *Dying For You*, which was being released in a week's time.

Kerri and Fox were both eighteen. Kerri was thin and pretty. The drums she played dwarfed her tiny body. Sapphire squeezed past her to get to the wardrobe.

"Saph, is there a spot on my neck?" Kerri asked, and Sapphire bent down to look.

"Who's gonna be able to tell from all that distance?" Fox said. The guitarist was leaning against the shower, messing around with his harmonica. Fox had long, straight, black hair and was almost as thin as Kerri. Sapphire had fancied him like mad since the first moment she saw him, at the auditions. Hud, however, had made the rules clear from the off: members of the band weren't allowed to date each other.

"If I've got a spot, *I'll* know," Kerri complained. "That's enough."

"Nothing there," Sapphire assured her. "You look great. You look better than Trudi Garth!"

At the mention of Trudi's name, there was a rustling noise from the direction of the wardrobe. Sapphire turned around. No one else seemed to have noticed the sound.

"Think we'll get to meet Trudi tonight?" Fox asked.

"You like her, don't you?" Kerri teased. "I'll bet you wouldn't know how to act if she were to appear at the door now, wishing us good luck. *Oh, Trudi Garth, you're my heroine! Oh, Trudi, can I lick your shoes?*"

"You've got to admit she's hot," Fox argued, as Sapphire reached into the wardrobe for her stage costume.

"I heard she's had plastic surgery," Kerri commented.

Suddenly, Sapphire's clothes seemed to jump back at her.

"Wh-*at*?"

A girl in a black jumpsuit leapt out of the wardrobe, brandishing what looked a lot like a knife. She began to swing the weapon around. Kerri screamed. The four members of the group backed against the walls of their cramped dressing room.

"There's no need for this," Fox said, trying to take command. "Come on, *calm down*. What's wrong?"

The girl was about fourteen, wore too much make-up, and had mad eyes.

"Where's Trudi Garth?" she demanded. "Where is she?"

"She's not arrived yet," Fox told her. "The Ghosts aren't on till last."

A vein rose up on the girl's forehead and began to quiver. She was still holding the weapon, which Sapphire saw was a screwdriver. Its shaft looked awfully sharp. Fox was edging his way to the door.

"Who are you?" the girl asked, looking slowly around, taking in each of them in turn. "What group is this?"

"We're Face To Face," Art told her. "This is our first gig."

The girl scrunched her face up. "You're no–bodies!" she announced. "I go to all the trouble to sneak in here, and you're nobodies! Where's Trudi Garth? I've got something for Trudi Garth. She stole my boyfriend!"

Fox glanced at Sapphire. They exchanged looks which said *this girl is completely off her head.* Sapphire nodded at the door. Fox reached over to open it. "Why don't I show you where to wait for her?" he said.

"All right," the girl told him.

"After you," Fox told her.

"No," she hissed, suspiciously. "After you."

The girl followed Fox out. Sapphire went into the corridor after them. Fox was pointing, saying, "The Ghosts have the biggest dressing room, number six, but I don't think they're here yet. Want me to take a look?"

"I can do it myself," the girl said. She walked ahead of Fox, hurrying to the room. Sapphire looked frantically around. No security in sight. If Fox was wrong, and Trudi Garth had already arrived, she was in big trouble.

"Where is she?" Art asked, poking his head out of room number one. "I've got security on the phone."

Sapphire pointed. The girl was trying the dressing-room door. Fox looked terrified.

"It's locked!" the girl cursed and Sapphire breathed a sigh of relief.

A security man was running down the corridor. Art pointed and, suddenly, the girl was gone, running behind the stage, out of sight.

"She's got a weapon!" Fox warned as the security man went after her. Sapphire was tempted to follow, to see what happened, but she was half-undressed and due on stage in a quarter of an hour.

The three of them went back into the dressing room.

"Hud warned us it'd be mad," Sapphire said.

"He didn't say anything about people wanting to kill us," Fox pointed out.

"She didn't want us, she wanted Trudi Garth," Kerri said. "Who knows? Maybe Trudi *did* steal her boyfriend."

Sapphire asked the guys to turn their backs as she got into her costume, a bodysuit so tight it took Kerri all her strength to zip it up for her. There was a knock on the dressing-room door. Art let Hud in. "What the hell happened?" he asked the manager. "How come she got into our dressing room?"

Hud shrugged. "The door shouldn't have been left open. I've made a complaint."

"They caught her, didn't they?" Kerri asked, nonchalant.

Hud looked embarrassed. "Actually, no. Seems

the girl got through a gap between backstage and one of the exit corridors. No one knows quite how. Security found a black jumpsuit and a sharpened screwdriver in one of the girls' toilets, but the girl herself was long gone. They're checking the security videos."

"But we all saw her," Sapphire pointed out. "We could identify her."

"Look," Hud said. "You're on in five minutes. Forget what just happened. We don't know what the girl's wearing. There are ten thousand people out there. Ninety-five per cent of them are girls aged twelve to sixteen. There's no way we're going to pick her out."

2

The venue felt like an aircraft hangar. The roar as the group went on stage was like a plane taking off. Then a voice announced their name, and the cheers faded. Nobody had heard of them. But all that was about to change.

Each of them was terrified. As the opening act, Face To Face would perform just two numbers. The first was named after the group itself and would be the lead track on their album. Each member took turns to sing a line of the lyric.

Hard, but sweet
So strong, heat
Don't trust me
Tragedy

Art laid down the synthesizer riff. Sapphire played the bass line, then stepped centre stage to sing the first words. Fox brought his head right up against hers before singing the next line. Their bodies touched. Then he pulled away and played a guitar break. Now it was Kerri's turn. The spotlight hit the drums and she played a little roll before singing her three words in a deep, soulful voice.

For the first time, Sapphire became aware of where she was. The arena was full and the audience were paying attention. They wanted to like the group. If the band blew it tonight, they had no one to blame but themselves. The spotlight hit Art, who gave the one word his all, lingering on all three syllables. Now the four of them were lit up in red, yellow, blue and gold. They sang the chorus.

Caught in the middle
Can't find my place
So circumstantial
It's no disgrace
I need a lover
Can take the pace
Got to meet you
Face to face

Then Sapphire heard it. A roar of approval. The audience liked them. They liked the song! She was so relieved that she nearly missed her next line.

The song was over before they knew it. Art left

the keyboards and took centre stage. He introduced the band in his lilting, Irish accent, then told the audience he'd like to play their first single, which would be in the shops a week on Monday.

"And this song is for each and every one of you girls out there," he said. The girls, taking their cue, screamed. Sapphire glanced at Fox, who was cringing. He and Art were poles apart. Fox had argued for a rock song as their first single, but Hud had insisted on a ballad: *Seduce the girls, then shake them up a little,* he'd told Fox. And Hud was proving to be right. As Art sang *Dying For You*, the audience hushed, only to erupt in screams and cheers at the end of each chorus. It was a triumph.

They rushed off stage, elated. Hud bounced around, congratulating them.

"Absolutely marvellous!" he told them. "I knew it'd go well but I never thought it'd go that well. We're talking number one. We're talking…"

"Don't get carried away," Art told him.

"I'm telling you, every one of those kids is going to rush out and buy that single, every last one of them!"

Sapphire was enjoying Hud's enthusiasm, but she could see that Fox was distracted. Then she saw why. There, wearing jeans and a shapeless sweater – a stark contrast to her sexy stage get-up – was Trudi Garth, lead singer of The Ghosts. And she was charging towards them.

Trudi grabbed Fox. "It was you, wasn't it? You

14

led that murdering psycho to my dressing room, didn't you?"

"I – I knew you weren't there," Fox told her in an uncertain voice.

Trudi slapped him across the face. "How *could* you know? How *dare* you?"

"Trudi, Trudi, calm down." This was Hud, moving rapidly across to protect his assets. "Fox did magnificently. He would have protected you like he protected the girls in the group. If it wasn't for his fast thinking…"

Hud had his arm around Trudi Garth's waist and was leaning in towards her. Sapphire found it hard to credit that the singer would let their manager get that close. Trudi exuded hardness. But she let Hud hold her.

"Honey, you need to get changed," Hud told her. "We don't want any photographers snapping you in your sloppies, do we? Come on." He led Trudi away. Hud seemed to know everybody in the business and they all seemed to respect him. Sapphire didn't know if that was down to admiration or fear. Hud was twice her age. She couldn't pretend to understand him.

"Are you all right?" she asked Fox.

He nodded. "A good thing Hud was there. He's a great guy, isn't he?"

"Great," Sapphire agreed. She looked around, waiting for their manager to leave Trudi's dressing room and join them. But he didn't.

3

The Ghosts were at the height of their success. They'd just had their second number one and were the most successful girl group for years. They played hard rock, interspersed with power ballads. Trudi sang most of the ballads, while Tina Toldeo took lead vocals on the fast songs. The gimmick was that Trudi looked like the rocker, dressed in leather, with chains and heavy make-up, while Tina looked demure. She had pale skin, long blonde hair, and often wore a dress on stage.

The smattering of boys in the audience were only there for The Ghosts. But Fox wasn't impressed by the band, not any more. Their rock songs were old-fashioned, he thought, the ballads too schmaltzy. What Face To Face were trying to do was more interesting. But maybe he was kidding himself. Last year, when he was in a college covers-band, he'd had posters of Trudi Garth on his bedroom wall. She was a big star and he was still a nobody.

Hud had insisted that Face To Face stay to watch The Ghosts' act. Fox didn't like to admit that he'd seen them before, twice. On their own tours, The Ghosts played harder rock and there were a lot more boys in the audience. Trudi was the star.

Tonight, though, the girls were mainly cheering Tina. Her rock songs went down a storm, while Trudi's ballads were received politely. The leather-clad singer looked angry as she left the stage.

"We're better than them," Hud told the band, as he drove them to the bed-and-breakfast where they were staying. "I'm telling you – now's the right time – the top spot's there for the taking."

They went to their rooms. The group got two doubles with single beds, while Hud had a room to himself. Fox would have preferred to drive back to their house in London than share a room with Art, but they were going on to Sheffield the next day and had their first radio interview in the morning. Hud didn't want them worn out by travel.

"By Christmas it'll be first class hotel rooms and girls queuing up outside," Art told Fox as they played pontoon, too wired to sleep.

"I'd settle for one girl," Fox said, remembering the moment on stage when he and Sapphire had pressed their faces around the same microphone. When they were recording songs or shooting a video, there was some sexual tension, but it felt manufactured. Last night, the sexual chemistry felt real, exciting. Fox wondered if Sapphire felt the same.

However, he had to remind himself, members of the group weren't allowed to date. It was a sacking offence – Hud had made that clear from the start, when they auditioned. Couples in bands upset the power balance and alienated the fan base, Hud said. To underline the point, he'd got an understudy for each member of the group, so that if someone was sacked or chose to leave, they could be replaced at a moment's notice. Fox had seen his understudy once, a lanky youth who bore a slight resemblance to him. Hud wasn't kidding.

"There's one thing about the band that intrigues me," the DJ said the following morning, after playing *Dying For You*. "I read that each and every one of you is an orphan. Is that right?"

"Nearly," Kerri said. "I've got a dad somewhere, but I don't think he knows that I exist. My mum died last year after a long illness."

"I was adopted," Fox admitted. "I don't know anything about my real parents, don't want to." He didn't mention the huge rows he'd had with his adoptive parents and how he'd ended up in care.

"And you?" the DJ asked Art.

"My parents were in a show band," Art said, his voice taking on a lamentful lilt. "I don't remember them. They died in a bus crash when I was two. I was brought up by nuns."

"And what about you?" the DJ quizzed Sapphire, after sympathizing with Art. "If you don't mind me asking."

"I do mind, actually," Sapphire said. "I have no parents, no past."

The DJ looked intrigued. "Is Sapphire your real name?" she asked.

"It is now," Sapphire said. That was all the DJ could get out of her.

Fox was also intrigued by Sapphire. She had the second best voice in the group and was by far the better-looking of the two girls, he thought. Kerri looked a little too tarty for him, whereas Sapphire had *class* written all over her. Her face was beautiful, but in a sincere, earnest sort of way. With or without the heavy make-up she wore in public, Sapphire was a sexy, smart English Rose. But Fox was only allowed to go near her when they were on stage.

For that night's concert, security was doubled. Video stills of the girl from the night before were circulated, but they showed little: a girl in a black jumpsuit, her straight, brown hair tied back. The members of Face To Face weren't much help in fleshing out her description. Even Fox, who'd got closest to her, couldn't swear that he'd recognize the screwdriver girl if he saw her again.

The Yorkshire crowd weren't as enthusiastic for the first song as Birmingham had been the night before. Then *Dying For You* won them over. Fox was worried. The band's format was indie rock meets classic pop. But *Dying For You* was so strong, and Art had such a good voice that, if they weren't careful, Face To Face would become a ballads band. Art, the frontman, would use the others as a stepping stone to a successful solo career like George Michael or Robbie Williams.

Fox had to stop that happening.

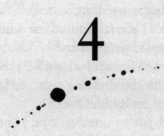

4

The last day of the tour was a Sunday. They'd done nine gigs in ten days, during which Face To Face had been in front of the audience for a grand total of seventy minutes. Their single had been getting steady but unspectacular airplay on commercial stations and teenage TV shows. Tomorrow, *Dying For You* would be released. Six days later, they'd know how they'd done in the only test that counted, the top forty chart.

When the group arrived at Wembley Arena, Art seemed strung out. He'd been looking more and more tense as the tour progressed. Sapphire wasn't surprised. If *Dying For You* failed, he would take the brunt of the blame.

The group were surprised to see a large press contingent waiting in the auditorium. They had the front row seats, not the ones up on the side, which the press usually occupied.

"What's going on?" Sapphire asked Hud.

"Trudi Garth's announced a press conference at seven o'clock," Hud told her. "The tabloids are on the scent of a big news story."

"Like what?" Kerri wanted to know. "She's carrying Prince William's baby?"

"I heard it was Michael Jackson's," Hud quipped, and they went to the dressing room to listen to the chart run-down on Radio One.

The DJ had got to number two. "And now," he said, "for the big question. There are two records left. One is last week's number one, and one is a new entry. So who's at number two?" There was a pregnant pause, before he whispered: "It's The Ghosts."

Sapphire gasped. The last two Ghosts' singles had gone straight in at number one. These days, if you weren't number one in your first week, you never would be. And the single, *Instant Affair*, was one of Trudi's songs. She'd be very upset. Sapphire wondered what her press conference was about.

"Let's go and take a look," Kerri suggested.

"I want to know what's going on," Fox admitted.

"Are you coming?" Sapphire asked Art.

He hesitated. "I think I'll just stay here. Collect my thoughts."

The three of them slinked to the side of the stage, where a table and two chairs had been set up. Trudi

Garth walked up the stage steps. She wore sneakers, an AIDS-awareness T-shirt and blue jeans – a far cry from her usual get-up. Even her hair was different, looser and plainer.

"What's she done to herself?" Sapphire asked Fox.

"I think she looks pretty," Fox said. "More like a real person." Sapphire felt a twinge of jealousy.

"I've got a brief announcement," Trudi said into the microphone. "After which, my manager will take a few questions, if you have them." She sounded clear, focused, like a newsreader, not a pop star. Trudi glanced at her notes, then spoke without looking at them again.

"Over the last few months, I've become increasingly disillusioned with the pop business. I've had all the success I've ever wanted, but it's only left me empty inside. The Ghosts started out as a real band, but ended up feeling like we were manufactured, like some cartoon group or, I dunno … Face To Face."

The three members of the group looked at each other in dismay. Sapphire couldn't believe it. Trudi had just dissed them in public. Was this about what had happened on the first night of the tour?

"I feel like my songwriting's been compromised and I've been forced into this image that doesn't reflect the real me. So I've decided to quit The Ghosts. I wanted to go out while we were on top, but I just learnt that we aren't. So, if you want to be cynical, you can call my leaving a protest against *Instant Affair* only getting to number two. That's all. Thanks."

"'Doesn't reflect the real me'," Fox quoted, snidely. "Her image used to be even more over the top before they had big hits. I'll bet that this is to do with Tina Toldeo being more popular than she is."

"I don't know," Sapphire said. "She looks gutted about something."

Trudi did look pretty upset as she walked backstage. She didn't look up, didn't notice that the members of the band she'd just slagged off had been watching her.

On stage, her manager was answering questions in a rapid fire voice. Was this connected with the fan who'd reportedly attempted to kill Trudi? No. Definitely not. Was she pregnant? Absolutely not. Had she fallen out with Tina Toldeo? No, they remained good friends. If they wanted to know how Tina felt about the decision, they'd have to ask her. Did Trudi have a solo contract? No. But yes, The Ghosts were about to sign a new contract and that might have affected Trudi's decision. No, the singer wasn't under contract to him, or anybody. After tonight, Trudi was a free agent. She never had to play or sing another note unless she wanted to.

"Think we'll feel like she does in a couple of years' time?" Sapphire asked Fox.

He gave her his *whatever* look. "If we're still doing this in two years' time," he said, "that'll do me. You know, success is about compromise. Hud explained that to me." He paused, then shook his head incredulously. "I can't believe that Trudi slagged us off like that. She doesn't even know us!"

In the dressing room, they told Art what had happened. His face was pale, but he didn't act too bothered.

"Fans aren't going to stop buying our single because Trudi doesn't like us," he said. "You've heard them every night. We're going to do fine."

"Anyway," Kerri put in, "what she said was true. We *are* a manufactured band. Hud got us together. But there's no shame in that. Boy groups and girl groups don't form naturally – you need too much money to launch them. All right, so The Ghosts met at university, then dropped out and made a go of it. But they're the exception that proves the rule. What matters is whether our music is good. Right?"

"Right!" they chorused.

There was a knock on the door.

"C'mon," Sapphire said. "Let's go out there and knock them dead!"

5

Afterwards, the performance felt like a kind of dream, it was so hard to credit what had happened. Fired up by Trudi's remarks, the band gave their two numbers everything. The first song went down a storm, and when Art announced their first single, there was a high-pitched scream of anticipation. The audience knew the song already. They were waiting to hear it. They would rush to buy it. Art sang the lyrics that he had helped to write.

It's a crazy notion
We could go so high
Unleashed emotion
Don't let it go by

Never felt like this
You do it to me
Just one sweet kiss
Then baby you'll see

That I'm dying for you
Can't live if you're not near
Oh yes, I'm dying for you
Kill me if I'm not sincere

As he sang the final chorus, Art seemed to get really carried away. He clutched the microphone close to his heart. You couldn't hear the words properly. It didn't matter. The screams from the girls would have drowned the lyric out anyway. *He's some performer*, Sapphire thought, as Art took a step backwards and dropped to his knees. At first, Sapphire thought that Art was doing a classic star pose. It was really showy stuff. They hadn't rehearsed this. Art swooned.

Then, in front of 12,000 screaming fans, Art keeled over completely. He'd collapsed.

Sapphire stopped playing and ran over to the stricken singer. Fox got there as she was trying to lift his head.

"Do you think he's fainted?" Sapphire yelled at him.

Fox slapped the singer about the face, then started giving him mouth-to-mouth. Sapphire was aware of Kerri running over from the drums. She tried to get a pulse from his wrist, but felt nothing. That didn't mean anything. Sapphire had no first-aid training. The microphone lay next to the collapsed singer. Sapphire picked it up, then realized that it could be live. But it wasn't. Art hadn't been electrocuted.

"Someone fetch a doctor!" she yelled into the mike. "He needs a doctor now!" For the first time, Sapphire was aware of the audience's reaction. They were hysterical. Screams of delight and desire had turned into screams of distress and dread. Somebody brought the house lights up. Two people from St John's Ambulance Brigade came on with a stretcher. The other members of Face To Face followed their lead singer off the stage.

The doctor wouldn't let them into the treatment room, but his stern expression showed that it was serious.

"I think he stopped breathing!" Fox said, for the third time.

"Wait here," the nurse told him. "We'll let you know as soon as we have an idea what's wrong with him."

Fox turned to Sapphire. They clung to each other. On the other side of the door, the doctor worked on Art. Hud tried to go in, but was refused entry.

The other groups came and waited, too. Sapphire

was vaguely aware of whispered discussions about when to continue the show. A decision waited on the doctor's report. It didn't take long. The door opened.

"Are there any relatives here?" the doctor asked. "Next of kin?"

Hud shook his head. "We're his family," he said, melodramatically.

The doctor frowned. "The ambulance will be here any moment," he told the manager, "but there's nothing the hospital can do for him."

"He's only nineteen!" Sapphire protested. "He can't be…"

The doctor shook his head. "If it's any comfort, he didn't suffer. He died almost immediately, out there on stage."

6

The funeral took place on Saturday, six days later, in the small Irish town where Art had been born. Despite the remoteness of the place, nearly a hundred fans congregated outside the church. Many stars from the tour were there, though not Trudi Garth. The rest of the final concert had been cancelled, so Trudi had been denied her swansong with The Ghosts. There'd been huge publicity about Art's death, too, which had completely overshadowed the news about Trudi leaving the group.

The service was long and heartfelt. Many people there had known Art since childhood. Some had been friends of his parents, who'd died in equally tragic circumstances. Several nuns from the orphanage where Art grew up were also there. Fox, who'd felt unloved all his life, found this outpouring of emotion hard to take. How many people would show up at his own funeral, he wondered?

After the service came the burial. Light rain fell like spittle on the shining casket. Sapphire and Kerri each put a single red rose on the coffin before it was lowered. Then the fans were allowed to throw in their tributes: flowers, poems, even a teddy bear. Finally, the priest said a few words and Fox threw the first piece of earth. He didn't know why he had volunteered for the task. At last it was over.

One of the nuns came over and spoke to Sapphire. She seemed to think that Sapphire was Art's girlfriend, maybe because she'd been crying so much during the service. Fox didn't hear what they talked about. He thanked the fans for coming. Some were Irish, but most had travelled from England. They were kids who'd seen Face To Face on the *Smash Hits* tour. Fox was impressed by their restraint. Not one asked for an autograph. They were there because they'd adored Art, not him.

Then they were in the car returning to the airport. Sapphire looked distracted. She waited until they were out of sight of the village before turning to Hud and asking: "Did you know that Art had a heart condition?"

Hud looked shocked. "No, of course not."

"The nuns knew all about it. He was diagnosed at birth, one of them told me. They didn't expect him to live."

"He kept it to himself," Hud protested. "He passed a medical. How was I to know?"

"He had a hole in his heart!" Sapphire announced. "He should never have been doing something as stressful as appearing on stage."

Hud reached over and put his hand on Sapphire's knee. She brushed it away. "His death was as big a shock to me as it was to you," Hud said. "Art chose to lie about his condition. According to the preliminary autopsy report, the hole was tiny. Art probably thought that it had healed up and didn't want to lose his chance of being a star because of a childhood illness. No one could have predicted…"

"If you'd given him a proper medical, maybe they would have done," Sapphire said. "Mine lasted five minutes and the doctor was only really interested in the drugs test, making sure I wasn't on crack or heroin."

"He was only nineteen!" Hud argued. "How was I to guess that he'd had a heart condition all his life when he was determined to keep it hidden?"

"That's enough," Fox said. Recriminations would get them nowhere. "The question is, what are we going to do next?"

"It's too early to talk about that," Sapphire said. "We're mourning."

Fox didn't agree with her. Sapphire hadn't been especially close to Art. Fox was the one who'd shared a room with him, who'd played pontoon with him until two in the morning nine nights in a row.

"I reckon that Art would have urged us to go on," he said. "All Art wanted was to be a star. He wouldn't want us to lose our chance because of what happened to him."

"Maybe you're right," Kerri said.

"Of course he's right," Hud told the three of them. "The understudy will take Art's place. But we won't announce it for a couple of weeks, out of respect. We'll have to get him to re-record Art's vocals on the album."

"No!" Sapphire shouted. "That's obscene."

"Just a thought," Hud said, shrugging.

"With Art gone," Kerri pointed out, "we might not have a career. Think about it: with all the publicity about Art, the media don't think of us as a group of four equals. They see us as a dead singer's backing band."

It was a ghoulish notion. Now would be the time, Fox thought, for the three of them to go back to their families and lick their wounds for a few days. But none of them had families to go to.

The next day they found themselves in the London house which Hud had rented for them, waiting for the first singles chart that they were eligible to appear in. They had a rehearsal with Art's replacement on Monday morning, but they didn't even know his name yet. Hud wanted to come over for the chart run-down, but the group asked him to stay away. No matter how well the single did, the success would be Art's, not theirs.

Fox and Kerri sat together in the living room, listening to the chart show. The DJ was up to number three, and their song had still not appeared. Fox went to look for Sapphire.

"What's wrong?" he called, when she didn't answer her door. No reply. He knocked again, then tried the door. It was open.

A radio played quietly in the background. Fox had to strain to hear the words. *And holding on for a second week at number two, it's The Ghosts with what will be their last single featuring the original line-up.*

Sapphire was in bed, fully clothed. She hadn't been crying, but looked tired and depressed. To Fox, Sapphire seemed surprisingly young and vulnerable. He wondered how old she really was. Sapphire never talked about her past, her background. She gave the impression that she'd run away after being brought up in a children's home. Fox knew how awful most of them were. Unless you were really strong, they could screw you up for life.

"I feel guilty," Sapphire said.

"Why? What for?"

"For feeling so rotten. I know the single might do brilliantly, but it doesn't mean anything. We're washed up, can't you see?"

"We might be," Fox told her. "It's too early to say."

"And that's why I feel guilty – because I'm more upset about my career finishing before it's started than I am about Art. I'm horrible."

"Not horrible," Fox said, sitting down next to her on the bed. "I think you're a beautiful person. I think you're being over-sensitive, that's all. We're all worried about what'll happen to the band. That doesn't mean we aren't badly hurt by what happened to Art."

As the final run-down began, he held her. Maybe he would have kissed her, too, but Kerri came bounding up the stairs and they pulled apart.

"I don't want to hear this on my own," Kerri said. "Turn it up, turn it up."

"And now," said the DJ, "for our brand new number one. It's been a tragic week for this group. All our sympathies go out to the members of Face To Face. Here they are, with a song featuring their late lead singer, Art Taylor. *Dying For You*, the UK's new number one!"

7

The stranger was tall and well built, yet, despite his blue eyes and cute, close-cropped hair, oddly anonymous-looking.

"This is Chris," Hud told the group on Monday morning, "your new lead singer."

"What's with this *lead singer* business?" Fox asked. "The idea was that we all sing. Art was the keyboard player, remember?"

But not a very good one, Sapphire thought. Session musicians had done all the keyboard pieces for the album.

"I play piano too," Chris said. He walked over to the organ in the corner of the rehearsal room and turned it on. As Chris launched into *House of the Rising Sun*, Sapphire got a good look at him. He had classic boy-band good looks, she decided. As a poster boy, he was much more appropriate than Art had been. And his keyboard playing was brilliant. Then he began to sing. Sapphire shuddered. Compared with Art, Chris's voice had nothing. It wasn't bad, just anonymous, like his looks. Hear him on the radio and he could be from one of a half-dozen boy bands.

"I didn't mean to say *lead*," Hud apologized, when Chris finished. "You're a group of equals. I guess I thought of Art as a lead singer, but…" His voice trailed off. Sapphire noticed a flicker of satisfaction cross Fox's face.

"Look," Chris said, standing up and showing off his biceps. "I know this is a terrible time. Hud's had me under contract for months, like the rest of you, but if you don't want me in the band, I'll walk away."

The other three looked at each other. If it wasn't Chris, it would be someone else, they all knew that. They'd come too far to give up now, so they might as well get on with it. Each of them nodded.

"Let's give it a go," Kerri told Chris.

Hud had been working out a revised strategy. He offered a compromise over re-recording Art's vocals. Chris would redo the two songs that were down to come out as their second and third singles, but Art's vocals would be left on the rest of the album.

"It saves money and shows respect," Hud said.

Sapphire noticed the order in which he'd made those points.

"I think we should drop *Dying For You* from our stage set," she said. "Also as a mark of respect."

"I agree," Fox chipped in.

Kerri said nothing, but Hud was outraged.

"*Dying For You*'s a number one! It's a show-stopper! You can perform it as a tribute to Art."

"That'd feel ghoulish," Sapphire said. "Also – nothing personal, Chris – but Art had a very individual voice. You wouldn't sound right singing it."

"I wouldn't *feel* right," Chris said. "Not yet, any-way, while I'm still stepping into a dead man's shoes. Why don't we see how it goes? If the fans really want us to play the song, they'll let us know."

"If we still have any fans," Sapphire said.

"On that point, I have some news for you," Hud told them. "You know those cards that we put in the singles – so fans could send off and join the mailing list or fan club? We've had over fifty thousand returned. Twenty thousand of them want to pay money to join the fan club!"

Fox punched the air triumphantly.

"I'm telling you," Hud announced, "this is only the beginning!"

8

The video for the second single was being shot in secrecy. The original plan had been to use film from the *Smash Hits* tour, but Art's death had ruled that out. Instead, the director was shooting the band walking in Regent's Park, intercut with footage of the group playing to an imaginary audience.

They had to be there early, before many people were in the park. It was cold, and there was a lot of waiting around. One journalist had been granted an exclusive "behind the scenes" interview. It would be the group's first since Art's death, seven weeks before. Hud had given them strict instructions on what to say and what not to say. The journalist had been warned that they were still too upset to talk about Art's death in any detail. Still, she tried it on.

"Was one of you particularly close to Art?" she

asked Kerri and Sapphire, while the boys were being filmed.

The girls looked at each other and both shrugged. "We were all very fond of each other," Sapphire said, tactfully.

"The way you rushed over to him when he collapsed," the journalist said. "It looked very..."

"Sapphire got there first because she was the nearest," Kerri answered for her. "But, you know, one of the things the group agreed when we started was that we wouldn't date each other. It could cause all sorts of problems. And we've stuck to that."

"Isn't that rather *unnatural*?"

"We prefer to call it *professional*," Sapphire said.

They were called to do their spot walking together. The video's concept went like this: Sapphire and Kerri were out walking in the park when they bumped into Chris and Fox. You saw them having a laugh together, which led to their forming a group. It was all to be done very innocently. The director said she wanted it to look like the title sequence of *Friends*.

"Just chat to each other naturally," the director said. "I'll tell you when we've got enough."

There was a sudden burst of light from a cluster of trees. The director swore.

"I'll sort it," Hud said. The manager ran over and chased off the photographer lurking there. Sapphire recognized the guy, maybe because he was nice-looking. Alan Mackay was one of a group of tabloid photographers who were always hanging around the group's house, trying to get a candid shot. He was the youngest of them, and would flirt with Sapphire and Kerri given half a chance. But Mackay wasn't that good at composing a photograph. Working freelance, he didn't get many photos in the papers. So he chased the group even more.

Once Alan had been seen off, the girls walked arm-in-arm. In the real world, Sapphire and Kerri had somehow failed to become close friends. Since the tour, the two had spent little time alone together. It was Sapphire's fault, she knew. Art's death had made her withdraw into herself. She explained this to Kerri as they walked for the cameras.

"Oh, don't be daft. I understand," Kerri said. "I seriously considered quitting myself. If I'd had somewhere to go…"

"Me too," Sapphire said.

"Cheer up," the director called. "You're meant to be having fun!"

"It's too cold to be having fun," Kerri replied.

"*Pretend!* Talk about sex, or something."

They walked on. "When'd I find time to have a sex life?" Kerri asked.

"Ditto," Sapphire said. "Mind you, you do seem to spend a lot of time talking to Chris."

"He's cute, isn't he? If he wasn't in the group…"

Sapphire grinned. "But rules are rules."

They giggled.

"That's more like it," the director called.

"Chris thinks that you and Fox are getting it together," Kerri said.

"I wish," Sapphire said. "I guess we're kind of tight but … an opportunity like this only comes along once. I'm not going to mess it up because I fancy some guy."

"That's what I told Chris. You know what he said? *It's all pretend – as long as we act single in public, it doesn't matter what we do in private. Hud isn't going to sack anybody. That's all bluff.*"

"I'd rather not take the risk," Sapphire said. Then she read between the lines of what Kerri was telling her. "Chris made a pass at you, didn't he?"

Kerri started giggling again. "I guess he did."

"And did you?"

Kerri glanced down the footpath, where Fox and Chris were waiting to "accidentally" bump into them. They weren't in earshot.

"Not yet," she said. "I was sorely tempted – I mean, I'm eighteen and I haven't had a boyfriend for a year!"

"Brilliant, girls!" the director called out.

"Oh, God," Sapphire said, "I've just had a thought."

"What?" Kerri asked.

"All the things we've been saying. Suppose a lip-reader watches the video? All our secrets will be out!"

Kerri burst into hysterical giggles.

"That's even better," the director called. "Keep it up!"

9

"**H**ave you seen this?" Fox said angrily, throwing the tabloid newspaper on the dressing-room floor. Sapphire picked it up. *This* was an interview with Trudi Garth, entitled: *Why I Quit by rock's sexiest siren.* Sapphire skimmed it.

"It's more or less the same as she said at the press conference."

"Read the penultimate paragraph."

Sapphire did.

"You have to be cynical about the motives of everybody in the business," Trudi says. She even casts doubts about the death of Face To Face vocalist, Art Taylor. *"It wouldn't surprise me if the manager knew he had a heart condition when he hired him. Face To Face are a complete con. They're a totally manufactured group. They say they write their own songs, but that's garbage."*

"That's slander!" Sapphire said.

"Libel," Kerri pointed out.

They called Hud over. He'd already seen the article.

"Sticks and stones," he said.

"We ought to sue," Fox told him.

"Don't you mean that I ought to? It's me and the record company she's getting at." Hud laughed. "Nah, I know Trudi. She's an impulsive girl. This is obviously sour grapes. Anyone reading it will understand that."

"Couldn't you sue the paper?" Sapphire asked.

"And get all the British tabloids against us? No thanks. We need them more than they need us. Now, are you ready to go on stage?"

Tonight, they were doing a secret gig for members of the Face To Face fan club, reintroducing the band to live performance. It would also give the video director more convincing footage for their second promo video.

The venue was a small London theatre, which was full to overflowing. This was the first time that Face To Face had played to an audience who'd come specifically to see them. It was also their first full-length set. They'd be playing the whole of the forthcoming album (except *Dying For You*) which lasted fifty minutes, together with two songs that they'd recorded for B-sides.

As they ran on stage, Sapphire realized that they hadn't agreed who'd be making the stage announcements. It couldn't be Kerri, because she was almost invisible behind the drums. It couldn't be Chris, because he was new. So it had to be her or Fox, who was still strapping on his guitar. As the crowd cheered, she stepped up to the microphone, unsure what words would come out of her mouth.

"Thanks for coming," she said, then paused. "We're all really nervous," she added. The audience seemed to quieten down. They were willing her to succeed. "I want to introduce Chris," she said, pointing at the youth standing behind the keyboards. "He's even more nervous than the rest of us."

The crowd obliged with a mighty cheer. *It's going to be all right*, Sapphire told herself. Then she remembered the other thing she ought to say.

"I don't know if anyone's already explained, but we're shooting a video." More cheers. "So we're going to do the new single first, before our hair gets messed up and all that." Laughs. "In fact, we'll be doing it twice. The first time, we'll mime to a tape, just so that we get the timing exactly right. Then we'll play it live. In fact, we're going to play you every song we've recorded." More cheers. "But now, I want you to go crazy. Remember, you're going to be on TV!"

The tape began and the audience played their part. Sapphire felt oddly detached. It was weird, pretending to play in front of all these screaming fans. Girls pressed forward at the front of the stage, throwing flowers, notes… One of them looked familiar. Sapphire remembered the girl in the black jumpsuit. Was it her? There'd been so many girls on the tour. Their faces all blurred into one. The song came to an end. Sapphire grinned at Fox, then nodded at the microphone. He stepped forward.

"All *right*! Now you know what the song sounds like, we're really gonna play it!"

They launched into *Face To Face*. Suddenly, everything worked. After weeks of mourning, they were a proper band again. Chris's keyboard sound really bolstered the song. All Sapphire's doubts were gone. They played every number they knew, and more. Each of them had one lead vocal, and those songs went down as well as the numbers where they all sang. At the end, the audience wouldn't let them stop. They hadn't planned an encore, but performed *Face To Face* once more, with the cameras still rolling. Then they came back on for the last time, arms around each other, like actors taking a curtain call.

When they came off stage for the final time, Sapphire found a sharpened screwdriver sticking into the door of the girls' dressing room.

10

"Security!" Kerri called. "Where's security?"

The director came running backstage. "That was tremendous," she said. "The encore, sweat pouring all down you, was *stupendous*! That's the one I'm going to use for the video. In fact, maybe we should put out a video of the whole performance." She paused, sensing the girls' discomfort. "Is something wrong?"

"Somebody got backstage," Sapphire said.

"When?" the director asked, then saw what Sapphire was pointing at and shuddered. A moment later, the theatre's security chief arrived and took a look at the screwdriver.

"It wasn't there ten minutes ago. I've been doing regular checks on this area."

"Would you look inside the dressing rooms, please?"

"Of course."

Sapphire was dripping sweat and beginning to shiver. Even so, neither she nor Kerri dared go in.

"Did you get a lot of film of the audience?" she asked the director.

"Yes. Especially the ones at the front."

"I'd like to look at the film as soon as possible. I thought I recognized someone."

"All clear," said the security chief, coming out of the dressing room. "Probably someone's idea of a joke."

"No joke," Hud said, joining them. "We're going to take this very, very seriously indeed. But for now, get yourselves washed and rested. I've booked us a table at the River Café. That was a performance to celebrate!"

Lianne joined her boyfriend in the slow moving queue to leave the theatre.

"What happened to you?" he asked. "You know, they did another encore. It was brilliant. They…"

"I needed the loo and I thought they'd finished," she interrupted him.

"All right if we queue for autographs?" he asked, smiling sheepishly. She loved that smile. "I guess so," Lianne told him. "So, tell me, now that you've seen her in the flesh, do you still think that Sapphire's better-looking than Trudi Garth?"

"You bet!" Jem said. "You know, she's younger, sexier and she's got a better voice. Anyway, Trudi's retired. But what did *you* think? Were they better than when you saw them before?"

Jem had given her his ticket for the NEC gig. He couldn't use it because he'd had food poisoning. Where he'd got it from was a mystery. It couldn't have been the shepherd's pie that Lianne cooked in home economics. After all, she'd eaten some, too, and had been fine afterwards.

"They've come on a lot," Lianne said. "That Irish guy could sing, but I fancy his replacement far more." She paused. "Not jealous, are you?"

Her boyfriend grinned. "It's only fantasy, innit? Harmless stuff."

"Harmless," Lianne agreed.

There was a big crowd around the stage door. A thirty-something guy in a baseball cap opened it. Behind him was a photographer, taking snaps of the fans. Lianne dropped her head. She didn't want to be recognizable.

"Hi," the guy said. "My name's Hud. I'm Face To Face's manager. Look, I'm really sorry about this. Kerri, Sapphire, Fox and Chris would love to meet their fans and sign as many autographs as you want, but we've had a serious security alert and everybody's a bit shaken up. I'm sure you'll under-stand that we can't take any chances. So, thanks for coming, but please, leave now. Next time, I promise."

Obediently, the crowd left. "Let's go," Jem said to Lianne.

"They'll be out in a minute," Lianne argued. "With everybody else gone, you'll be able to get an autograph without queuing. You can tell Sapphire how much you love her."

"And she'll think that I'm some creep who wouldn't go away when her manager asked me to. No, thanks. Come on, let's go."

Lianne slipped her hand into his and they walked towards the tube station. Lianne kept a smile on her face, but, inside, she was seething. Jem was smitten. Sapphire was going to have to watch herself.

"There!" Sapphire said, pointing at the blonde girl on the right, near the front of the stage. "She's the one."

"How can you be sure?" Chris asked.

"I'm pretty sure," Sapphire said, turning to Kerri and Fox. "What do you think?"

"Could be," Kerri said. "But I didn't get a really good look at her before."

"There's a definite resemblance," Fox agreed. "But if she's there, how could she get backstage?"

"Fast forward the film," Sapphire told the director.

As the show built to a climax, the director had ordered frequent shots of the crowd's mounting hysteria. During the first encore, the blonde girl was still there. She seemed less manic than the other people at the front, who were mostly girls. The director fast-forwarded to the second encore.

"Look!" Sapphire said, excitedly. "She's gone!"

"She might be in the loo," Kerri said.

"Or she might have fainted, been carried out," Chris suggested.

"No," Hud said. "I checked with the medics. No girl of that description needed treatment."

"Let's match her picture against the girl at the NEC," Fox suggested. They did. If you looked at the video freeze-frame and compared it to the still image from the security surveillance tape, it *could* be the same girl – but her clothes were different, her hair shorter. The detail of her face was too grainy to be sure.

"I think it's the same girl," Sapphire said.

"What do we do if it is?" Fox asked.

"She hasn't actually hurt anybody," Kerri pointed out. "Maybe she just wants attention."

"Why's she following us?" Chris asked.

"She's seen me in my boxer shorts," Fox pointed out. "Maybe she's in love."

"I knew you were desperate for a girlfriend," Kerri said, "but I didn't think you were that desperate."

They laughed. Kerri could always turn things into a joke.

"Let's not lose any sleep over this," Hud said. "We'll take her seriously. I'll get us someone on security full-time, just to be on the safe side. But not a word to the press. We've got the second single out next week. Lots of positive publicity, that's the name of the game. Now, come on, I'm starving. Let's go eat!"

Outside, Alan the photographer was waiting. Hud held up his hand to muck up the pictures, but Alan Mackay wasn't holding a camera.

"I heard that you had some threats from a fan who got backstage," he said.

"No comment," Hud told him. "Now, we're in a hurry."

"Hold on," Alan urged. "I took a load of fan photos today for an article in one of the Sundays. I've got pictures of the fans in the theatre, queuing up to go in, and waiting by the stage door. Would you like me to print copies for you?"

"We would," Sapphire said, before Hud could reply. "Bring them to the house, please."

"I'll do that."

"You see," Sapphire said, once they were in the car. "The press aren't always against us."

"He'll want something in return," Hud told her. "Just you wait and see."

11

"Their first single was number one for seven weeks. Their second single came out this week and is bound to make a big impression on the charts this Sunday. Please welcome, live for the first time on *Top of the Pops*, Face To Face!"

This was more nerve-racking than appearing on stage, Fox realized. Millions of people were watching. The song only lasted for three minutes and forty-two seconds, but it felt like an hour. The group were so concerned about playing badly that their vocals were rough.

"Give it another go," the producer told them. "You're better than that."

"Sorry," Fox said into the microphone.

Luckily, the show was taped two days' in advance. You could keep doing the song until you got it right.

Ever since he was a kid, Fox had dreamed of being on *Top of the Pops*. In his dreams, he'd be fronting his own band, playing really cool rock music, not power pop like this. However what he was doing now was near enough. It was real.

They played the number again. The fans went wild again. This time, the producer seemed satisfied. The group headed back to the dressing room.

"Fox, can I have a word?" asked a pretty young woman as he was coming out.

"Sure."

He thought that she was going to ask for an auto-graph. All right, she looked five years older than him, but plenty of older women had made a play for Fox over the last few weeks. This one was gorgeous.

"Maybe I could buy you a drink?"

"Why not?"

As they headed off to the BBC bar, Fox saw Sapphire giving him a funny look. It was unfair, Fox thought, as he watched Chris, surrounded by teen-age girls. Women came on to him and Chris all the time, but male fans were scared to approach Kerri and Sapphire for more than an autograph.

The woman's name was Shirley. They talked for a while about the show and whether the single would hit number one. Shirley seemed to take control of the conversation. Fox found himself admitting that he didn't have a girlfriend. Shirley made it clear that she was interested in the role, for tonight at least. She was too old for him, Fox decided, as he got another round of drinks. And she reminded him of his one-time foster sister, who was bad news.

"I hear that you were adopted, is that right?" Shirley asked, when he returned with the drinks.

"Fostered. But I don't like to talk about that," Fox told her.

"But your foster parents threw you out. What was that all about?"

"I said I don't..."

Shirley put her hand on his knee to calm him down, and left it there.

"You know what they say? They say you stole from them, seduced their fifteen-year-old daughter and, when they got heavy with you, threw a party which ended up with their house being smashed to pieces."

"What is this?" Fox asked. "Are you a reporter?"

"Yes. With the *Sunday Mirror*. I said that when I introduced myself."

"Did *not*."

Shirley smiled superciliously. "It was noisy out there. You must have misheard. But the thing is, we're running an interview with the family you lived with, in Sunday's paper, and we want to give you the opportunity to tell your side of the story."

"Well for a start," Fox said, "I didn't..." Then he remembered all his training, and stopped himself. "Hud!" he yelled.

The manager came over from the bar, where he'd been drinking with the producer. "What is it?"

"This woman's from the *Sunday Mirror*. She's planning to print some malicious lies on Sunday."

"We'll see about that," Hud said. "Off you go, son. I'll deal with this."

At the other end of the bar, Kerri and Sapphire were hanging out with two members of one of Fox's favourite bands. He could tell that he wouldn't be welcome. And to think that a few minutes ago he'd been sorry for them. He went outside and took a taxi home alone.

The story duly appeared on Sunday. Hud had managed to remove one or two details, but the gist of it was that Fox was a bad lad who had wrecked their home and corrupted their convent-educated daughter.

"She was the one who corrupted me!" Fox protested, when the others teased him about it. "She was older than me. The party was her idea. I just did as I was told!"

"I'll bet you did," Chris said. "She's not bad-looking."

"If I were you, I wouldn't deny the stories," Sapphire said. "All the girls love a bad lad. Now your roles are defined. Chris is the goody-goody. You're the bit of rough."

"Neither confirm or deny," Hud ordered. "If the story affects Fox's popularity, we'll leak his side of it to a sympathetic journalist."

They listened to the chart run-down. This was not going to be a surprise. They knew how good their sales figures had been during the week. At a quarter to seven, the DJ rang and asked them to be ready to make a live comment.

"And at number two, last week's number one, *Rhianna*, by Paul Nelson. Which means that we have a new number one. And on the line with me now, I have all four members of Face To Face: Fox, Chris, Sapphire and Kerri. How does it feel to have your second single go straight in at number one?"

"Fantastic," Kerri said.

"Awesome," Chris said.

"Pretty damn cool," Fox told him.

"You know," Sapphire said, taking a deep breath, "a lot of people thought we were one-hit wonders and it's good to prove them wrong. So if you're listening, Trudi Garth, we wrote this all by ourselves. Let's see you do better!"

"*Ooh*," the DJ said. "A bit of good-natured rivalry there. But congratulations to Face To Face as their second single does just as well as their first, going straight in at…" The *number one jingle* played and the song began. The band whooped and cheered, but their enthusiasm was slightly forced. They'd known what was coming. It didn't feel real yet. When the song was over, Hud turned off the radio and sighed.

"Why on earth did you have to slag off Trudi Garth?" he asked Sapphire.

"She started it," Sapphire said.

"She did. And it made her look bad. Now you look bad, too. And you don't know Trudi. She really bears grudges."

"How come you know her so well?" Fox asked.

"I don't," Hud said, "but I used to. I managed The Ghosts for a few months when they were still a hard rock band, playing small college venues. I wanted to take them in a more commercial direction, but they were happy being the darlings of the trendy music papers. So they sacked me. Later, they realized I was right, made the change. So they've got respect for me."

"Why didn't you manage them when they changed their minds?" Kerri asked.

Hud gave a wry smile. "Hiring a new manager's like falling in love, timing is everything. Anyway, I've no regrets. If I were managing them, Trudi would still have left. They're in a mess now. Whereas I've got you guys. And you're going to be far, far bigger than they ever were."

The phone rang. Sapphire answered it, wondering who was calling to congratulate them.

"Sapphire?" said the voice at the other end.

"Speaking."

"I'm going to get you, *bitch*!"

"What? Is that Tr—"

But whoever was on the other end had hung up.

12

After the second number one, everything got scary. While *Dying For You* was at the top of the chart, the group had gone to ground: re-recording the album, shooting the video, rehearsing the stage show. But now they were doing radio appearances and TV spots all the time. Tickets for their first tour of the UK had sold out in a day.

Performing didn't scare them. Being on stage was what they looked forward to most. The scary thing was the people. Crank phone calls and letters were the least of it. Everybody they met wanted something from them: an interview, an autograph, a job even. Worst of all were the ones who wanted to be their friends.

It was all right, Sapphire thought, being back-stage at *Top of the Pops* meeting someone whose songs you knew. You were peers, you had something in common. What was weird was chatting to strangers who told you how great you were before they had a chance to get to know you. That kind of attention was exciting for a while, part of being a success. But the buzz soon gave way to a feeling of hollowness.

How did you relate to people when you were a star? How did you choose your friends? Sapphire wasn't from London. Her old friends were still at school or college. She'd deliberately lost touch. They probably didn't even recognize her now that she had a different name and a new image. Sapphire couldn't go back.

The rest of the band seemed to find it just as hard. Fox and Kerri both said how people they'd known for ages had started treating them differently. They couldn't relax around them any more. Only Chris had London friends who he still hung out with.

"It's hard to know how to behave," he said. "I've got two hundred quid in my pocket, so do I buy all the drinks? And most of my mates are in the business. They're trying to get a record deal, or a gig or whatever. If I talk about what it's like being in Face To Face, it sounds like I'm showing off. If I don't, it looks like I'm being standoffish. You can't win."

Inevitably, the band closed in on themselves. They might not naturally be the best of friends, but they became a family, living one huge private joke. It helped, Sapphire thought, that they weren't allowed to go out with each other. Sex didn't get in the way. After all, suppose she had a thing with Fox and it didn't work out? They'd still have to be around each other sixteen hours a day. That'd be awful.

The tabloid papers kept printing rumours about the group's love lives. Hud said that they had to put up with it. The stories were free publicity. Headlines had Sapphire going out with both Chris and Fox. She was also supposed to have been secretly engaged to Art before he died. One story also suggested that Chris and Kerri were an item.

Fox was usually described as a teenage Lothario, partly because of the stories about him and his foster-sister. He went to clubs sometimes, Sapphire knew. Occasionally, girls came back to the house with him. Sometimes he came home late, or not at all. Normal behaviour for an eighteen-year-old boy, Sapphire thought, though it made her jealous.

Sapphire herself had one admirer who the papers had no idea about. Jim was twenty-two, built like a middle-weight boxer, and looked like what he was: a fully trained bodyguard. He was assigned to the whole group, but spent as much time as he could with Sapphire. He kept hinting that, if he weren't on guard all the time, he'd like to spend even more time with her.

Sapphire was flattered. Jim wasn't her type, but he was good company, and part of her liked the idea of making Fox jealous. There was nothing to stop Sapphire seeing Jim. However, bodyguards weren't supposed to get romantically involved with their charges. Big Jim hinted that he didn't care about that: he'd risk his job if she gave him the nod.

"There's plenty of other work for a guy like me," he said.

But Sapphire didn't want to be responsible for Jim losing his job. How could she go out with him if he didn't work for the band any more? So she stayed celibate, and was only lonely when she retired to her hotel room at night. Even then, Jim was always only a door or two away.

One night, after a show in Glasgow, the bodyguard joined Sapphire, Kerri and Chris lounging on sofas in the plush hotel bar. Middle-aged conference delegates kept wandering past their table, trying to get a peek at the band. Now and then they were asked for autographs, always "for my daughter". A man of at least forty asked if he could have his photo taken with Sapphire. "Just to prove I met you," he said. Sapphire declined politely.

"You get some weird ones," she said when he'd gone.

"Better him than the screwdriver girl," Kerri commented.

"At least there's no sign of her on the tour," Chris said.

"You haven't played Birmingham yet, or London," Jim told them, cautiously. "Those are the places where she showed up before."

"That's one thing about being on tour," Sapphire said. "I've not been getting any crank calls."

They'd had to have their number changed in London after the band's home number was circulated on the internet. The *bitch* call had been the first of many.

"You've had plenty of odd calls," Jim said, "but the desk only puts them through if the callers identify themselves and they're on the approved list."

"Oh, great," Sapphire said. "So, if an old friend calls up, there's no way they can get in touch with me."

"They can leave a message," Jim assured her, "as long as it's not obscene."

"I didn't think you had any old friends," Kerri teased. "You're the girl without a past, remember?"

Sapphire laughed uneasily. She'd told the rest of the band a bit about her background, but was only comfortable with them knowing what she wanted them to know. Better that than telling lies.

"Watch out," Jim said, and pointed.

Chris looked round, then gave a relaxed wave. "It's only Alan," he said.

Alan Mackay had handed over his photos of the crowd at the fan-club performance. Unfortunately, they hadn't been much help. There were a couple of images showing someone who might have been the screwdriver girl, but one was out of focus, while the other only showed her back.

After that, the group owed him a favour. Alan was

always around their house or hotel, trying to get something he could sell. He was young and enthusiastic and didn't bother the band as much as some of the other photographers. It was still annoying, though, having someone in your face late at night. He waved at the band and wandered over, putting down his heavy camera bag on the sofa next to Sapphire.

"You're not meant to take pictures inside," Jim told him, not for the first time.

"Unless you give permission," Alan corrected him. "I'm skint. I need the money. And it's perishing out there. Mind if I join you for a drink?"

"Sorry," Sapphire said, "we're under strict orders from Hud. No fraternizing with the press unless someone from the record company's there."

"Ah, but *mein führer*'s gone to bed, hasn't he?" Alan said. "So, while the cat's away…"

Kerri got up. "I'm knackered," she said. "G'night."

Jim gave Sapphire and Chris a warning look, then saw her to her room.

"So tell me," Alan said, "who's sleeping with who tonight? Off the record, of course."

"Don't you have a home to get to?" Chris asked, ignoring the question. "It's pretty late."

"I sleep in my car," the photographer replied, adding, optimistically, "unless one of you guys has a spare bed."

"Is this man bothering you?" It was the hotel night-manager, alerted by Jim on his way upstairs. "I don't believe he's a guest."

Chris and Sapphire glanced at each other. They didn't want to be rude. Other people did that for them.

"I was just going," Alan said, quickly. "See you guys tomorrow."

They wished him good night. When Jim returned, Chris said good night, too. It was just before midnight. Sapphire wasn't tired yet.

"Want to play some cards, backgammon maybe?" she asked Jim.

"You're the boss. Here, or in your room?"

"Here's safer," she said, getting a travel backgammon set out from her bag. *Safe from what?* he could have asked. *Me?* But Jim was too diplomatic to make anything of it.

"Have you noticed something about Chris and Kerri recently?" Jim asked, as Sapphire laid out the counters.

"What?"

"They always go to bed within a few minutes of each other."

"Maybe they like to leave us alone together," Sapphire joked. If something was going on between Chris and Kerri, she'd rather not know.

"I've seen Chris in hotel corridors surprisingly early in the morning," Jim commented, as Sapphire threw the dice.

She sighed. "You're not going to tell Hud, are you?"

The bodyguard shrugged. "Not unless he asks

me. We all have secrets. They're not going to tell on you, either, if you want to have some fun…"

Sapphire gave him a *not in this lifetime* smile. "Your throw."

Jim won, and got to start. Sapphire played in silence, unsure what to say. Jim was several years older than her. Sapphire respected him. She didn't know how to turn him down any more considerately than she already had done. She didn't know if, sometime, she might change her mind. Female stars often dated their bodyguards or personal trainers. They were the only blokes able to get close to them on a regular basis. All Sapphire knew was that she wished Fox were here with her, not Jim.

"Best of three?" Jim asked, forty-five minutes later.

Sapphire shook her head. "Ready for bed."

"I'll see you upstairs, then."

Jim showed her to the door, watched her go safely in, then withdrew, the perfect gentleman. Sapphire was still in the bathroom ten minutes later when the fire alarm went off.

It was a horrendous racket, a high-pitched drone, designed to wake the deepest of sleepers. Sapphire pulled on her robe, grabbed her bag and ran into the corridor. She was one of the first out. All around her, she could hear the sound of stamping feet, panic. Jim was already in the corridor, wearing only his tracksuit bottoms. He was banging on Fox's door. One of the hotel staff came running along the corridor. Jim stopped knocking.

"Where's the fire?" he asked.

"Alarm was set off on the next floor up."

Jim turned to Sapphire. "If Fox opens up, make sure he's not got some bimbo with him. I don't smell smoke. This reeks of a photographer's set-up to me."

He ran after the porter, up the stairs. The corridor filled up and people started to go down to the lobby. A notice in all of the rooms warned not to use the lift in the event of fire, but Sapphire saw that the lift nearest her door was coming down. The person inside it must either be stupid, or know that it was safe.

Another porter came along, trying to get people to move downstairs. Sapphire collared him. "Could you open this door, please? My friend's not answering."

The porter knew who she was and let her in. A quick look around showed her that Fox's room was empty. A moment later, Jim put his head in. He looked angry.

"Fox isn't here," Sapphire told him. "I don't know where he is."

"It wasn't him they were after," Jim told her, as the alarm abruptly stopped sounding. "It was Kerri and Chris. That bastard Alan Mackay just snapped the two of them leaving the same bedroom together. He's probably on his way to the tabloids right now!"

13

"Surely it's not as bad as all that," Fox argued. He'd got in from a club at two-thirty, surprised that everybody was still up and about. All six of them were meeting in Fox's room: the band, Hud and Jim. "There've been rumours, after all."

"Rumours make the world go round," Hud said. "But confirmation of the affair will mess up our fan base. It's important that you're all single, available. If it weren't for Art dying, and if we hadn't re-recorded the album once already, I'd sack the pair of them this minute."

Chris and Kerri looked chastened. "How could you fall for a gag like that?" Hud added.

"It's my fault," Jim said. "I should have insisted that all our rooms were on the same floor. Then I'd have got to that damn photographer before he got to them."

"Too late for that now," Hud said. "I'll see if I can get a number for Alan Mackay. Tomorrow's tabloids have already been printed, so we've got a bit of time. Maybe I can buy him off. Jim, I might need you again tonight. Stay awake, will you?"

"Yes, boss."

"The rest of you get some sleep. Big show tomorrow night. Oh, and Chris, stay in your own room or I'll invoke all the penalty clauses in your contract. You've only been in the group five minutes, so, if anyone goes, it'll be you. Got that?"

"Yes, boss," Chris said, without a hint of irony. Hud left Fox's room.

"Can I come and talk to you?" Kerri asked Sapphire, her voice sheepish and scared.

"Course you can," Sapphire replied. "I can't see myself getting to sleep in a hurry."

Kerri flopped on the bed next to Sapphire.

"What a mess," she said.

"How long's it been going on?" Sapphire asked.

"Since the second night of the tour."

That was ten days ago.

"We've been really careful," Kerri went on. "Chris thought that Jim might have guessed."

"He had."

"Do you really think that Hud'll sack Chris?"

"He makes the rules," Sapphire said. "But I doubt it. If I know Hud, he'll find a way to stop the story getting out. But you'll have to cool it." Kerri burst into tears. Sapphire comforted her.

"Are you in love with him?" she asked.

"I don't know," Kerri said. "I don't think so. He's only the second bloke I've been with. How do you tell how serious it is?"

"No point in asking me," Sapphire told her. "I've never been in love."

"It's just that I get really lonely," Kerri said. "It wasn't so bad on the *Smash Hits* tour, when we were sharing a room."

"I know what you mean," Sapphire said. "I get lonely, too. Maybe we could share again."

"Then the press would put about that we're gay," Kerri said, her voice sour. "That'd really make Hud's day."

"Let them think what they want," Sapphire said. "What I want to know is why our private lives are so important. We're fantasy figures on a stage. We do our job, but off-duty, we're ordinary."

"Don't kid yourself," Kerri said. "We can never be ordinary again."

The next morning they were due to set off at ten, but everyone was still in bed. Jim put his head round Fox's door at five past.

"I'm off to collect Hud from a meeting. Get the others to shake a leg, will you? Band meeting when I get back."

"Why me?" Fox asked.

"Why not?"

Fox got up. He'd been to a good club the night before. There were no Face To Face fans there. It was the sort of place where, if anybody recognized him, they were far too cool to let on. Fox could relax. A local journalist who wrote for the *NME* had taken him. The journo wanted to do an interview with the band, if the editor would let him.

"*NME* readers aren't interested in teenage pop bands," the journalist said. "But I reckon you're a lot more than that."

"Our manager likes to control the press we do really closely," Fox had said. "But I'll try to persuade him." Fox had been reading the *NME* since he was ten. One of his biggest day-dreams was to be on the cover.

Fox called the front desk and asked them to send up copies of all the day's tabloids. Then he phoned the others' rooms, giving them Jim's message. The papers arrived and he flicked through them. No incriminating photos of Chris and Kerri. But there would be tomorrow, unless Jim had fixed it.

Would the story mess up the band's career? Fox didn't know. He was glad now that he hadn't made a move on Sapphire at any time in the last year. He'd been tempted and he guessed that she had, too. But he'd stuck to his contract. On the other hand, if Chris and Kerri got away with it, why shouldn't he and Sapphire?

Fox put a tracksuit on. He was still only half awake. Right now, a quick run around the hotel grounds would get his adrenalin going, pump some blood into his brain.

He took the lift down to the lobby. Two uniformed police officers were talking to the manager. Fox squinted out of the front door. No photographers around. Good. As he began to jog, an ambulance pulled in, its siren at full volume. Fox noticed a couple of hotel employees standing on the edge of the outdoor swimming pool. One of them was gesticulating towards the ambulance driver.

He took a closer look. There appeared to be someone in the pool. Fox thought of going over. He had a life-saving certificate. But the situation looked under control. Who'd go for an outdoor swim at this time of year? he wondered. It was bloody cold.

Fox jogged around the hotel once. It wasn't a pleasant run. Too many traffic fumes.

But the cold was waking him up. Fox slowed down at the pool again, watching as the two ambulance men began to prod the water with a long stick.

"What's going on?" Fox asked the hotel manager, who was watching.

"Some poor bugger's drowned himself."

They'd managed to hook the body and were dragging it in. As he watched, Fox was aware of a taxi pulling in at the front of the hotel. Hud and Jim were getting out of it. Fox ought to go over to them. They had a meeting. But he had a terrible feeling of foreboding. Gently, the ambulance men lifted the body on to the side of the swimming pool.

"Been dead for hours," one of them said. He turned the body over so that it was face-up, then asked the manager, "Recognize him?"

"I don't think he's a guest. They were all accounted for last night when we had the fire alarm."

"Can I see?" Fox asked.

The ambulance men looked at him cautiously, seeing not a rock star, but an anonymous teenager in a tracksuit. "Here come the police," said one of them. "It's up to them."

But the ambulance man didn't cover the body, and, as the men stood to greet the two police officers, Fox got a good look. The man's head had been bashed in, but he was still easily recognizable.

"And who are you?" the more senior policeman asked Fox.

"My name's Michael Foxton. I'm a musician. And I'm afraid I know who the dead bloke is."

"Who?"

"His name's Alan Mackay. He was a photo-grapher."

14

When Fox got upstairs, the meeting had already begun. The door was ajar and he walked in unnoticed. Everyone was intent on listening to Hud.

"There's nothing to worry about," Hud was saying. "The lad agreed a price for the film."

"How much?" Chris asked.

"We made him an offer he couldn't refuse," Jim said, jokily.

"But I warn you," Hud added, "it's coming out of your royalties."

"Where is the film?" Chris asked.

"Destroyed," Jim said. "I watched him take the film out of the camera and do it himself."

"That might have been a mistake," Fox interrupted. "The film was evidence." All five turned round, noticing him for the first time.

"What's the problem?" Hud asked.

"I think the police'll be after the film," Fox told him. "You see, Alan Mackay's just been fished out of the hotel pool. He's dead."

"You're joking!" Chris said.

"That's not funny," Sapphire mumbled.

"I wish I was kidding," Fox said, and, this time, they seemed to believe him. Kerri burst into tears. Sapphire looked stunned. Hud turned to Jim.

"You gave him the money, yeah? Fifty grand."

"That's right. I met him in his car, just before four."

Hud didn't seem convinced. "You're sure you didn't decide to keep the money for yourself and get rid of Mackay another way?"

Jim looked affronted. "What do you take me for? I followed orders. The toerag probably decided to get drunk and fell in the pool."

He'd have trouble getting a drink at four in the morning, Fox thought. Hud turned to Fox. "What have you said to the police?" he asked tersely.

"Nothing," Fox protested. "I mean, virtually nothing. I said he'd been following the band around. I didn't mention him taking the picture of Chris and Kerri. After all, I wasn't there at the time."

Hud put his head in his hands. "We've got to work out how to spin this. It'll be hard to make it look like his death wasn't related to the band. First, we'd better make sure that you all tell the same story. Jim, run over the events of last night, would you? Let's see if we agree on them."

But before the bodyguard could start, there was a knock on the door. A man in a loose suit came in, accompanied by a smartly-dressed young woman.

"I'm DI Parker from Glasgow Serious Crimes Squad. This is DC Wordsworth. We're here about a man whose body has been recovered from the hotel swimming pool. This young man —" he pointed at Fox — "tells me that you have some knowledge of him."

Jim looked at Hud, who shrugged. "It's me you want to talk to," Jim said, sullenly. "I may have been the last person to see him alive."

"In that case," the DI told him, "you'd better come with us."

The others were asked not to leave the hotel until they'd been interviewed.

"But they've got a gig in Carlisle tonight!" Hud protested.

"We should be through with them by then," the DC told him politely.

When they'd gone, Hud was furious. "Why'd you have to bring the police straight here?" he asked Fox.

Fox was incredulous. "Hud, a guy was *killed*! I wanted to help."

"You could have given us time to sort ourselves out."

"What's to sort out?" Fox asked. "We tell the truth, including how Jim paid him off for the picture. You believe Jim, don't you?"

"Of course," Hud said. "If Jim was going to do someone in, he'd dump the body in a place a lot more clever than the hotel pool."

This answer didn't comfort Fox much. He and Sapphire exchanged concerned glances.

"I'm going to get some sleep before the shit really hits the fan," Hud said. "I've been up all night. If the police need me, I'll be in Jim's room."

"We're meant to check out in half an hour," Chris pointed out.

"I'll sort that. I don't want anyone leaving the hotel, OK?" Hud said, getting up to leave. "And no talking to the press, not a word."

"There's this journalist from the *NME* coming to the gig tonight," Fox began to say, then regretted opening his mouth. He wanted to add that they could use a sympathetic reporter on their side, but Hud didn't let him finish.

"Especially not the *NME*," he said.

They were left alone.

"What do you think happened?" Kerri asked.

"You don't think that Jim…?"

All three of them looked at Sapphire. She was the member of the band who was closest to Jim.

"No, I don't," she said. "I expect it was an accident."

"It didn't look like an accident to me," Fox said. "It looked like somebody attacked him, then dumped his body in the water."

"We've all got separate rooms," Chris pointed out. "We don't have alibis."

"Don't be ridiculous," Sapphire said. "It won't come to that."

"Why not?" Kerri said. "Somebody killed him. But you're wrong, Chris. You see, Sapphire and I do have an alibi – each other. I stayed in her room last night."

Chris met Fox's eyes reluctantly. "I didn't have a motive," Fox said.

But Chris did. There was a knock on the door: DC Wordsworth.

"I'd like a word with Chris Henderson, please," she said, then added, "alone."

That left three of them.

"Chris couldn't have done it," Kerri said. "Why would he have done? He knew that Hud was sending Jim to pay Alan off."

"Suppose Chris got to him first?" Sapphire said. "He's a big lad, bigger than Alan. He could have beaten Alan up when he refused to hand over the film, dropped him in the pool. Maybe Jim's lying to protect Chris."

"This is *Chris* we're talking about," Kerri pointed out. "He's not like that. God, I wish I'd stayed in his room all night."

"The question we have to answer," Fox said, "is what Alan was doing back at the hotel. Why wasn't he on his way to a newspaper or somewhere he could get his photos developed?"

"He must have been meeting Jim," Kerri said.

"Maybe he was killed for the money," Fox speculated. "There are rough areas round here. Fifty thousand's a lot of cash."

"Presuming that Jim handed it over," Kerri said. "How did he get his hands on fifty thousand quid in the middle of the night anyway?"

Fox and Sapphire had to agree that that was a good question.

15

Lianne walked into the hotel, past the police officers and the journalists who were starting to arrive. The group were meant to have gone by now. She'd been hidden in their tour bus since five this morning, waiting. The photographer's murder must have mucked things up for them.

But not for her.

Lianne walked straight in through the staff entrance. Face To Face always stayed at hotels in this chain. That had been easy to find out. The layout of these hotels was always the same. She'd researched them, too. Had even spent a day working as a chambermaid at the one in her home town. Lianne knew where to find a uniform, and changed into it. Then she headed up to the fourth floor.

A quick glance at the mirror in the lift told

Lianne that she looked innocuous. Jem sometimes told Lianne that she was beautiful. Lianne knew that, without make-up, she was plain, ordinary. But she was turning that to her advantage. People rarely remembered her.

Last night, she'd persuaded the photographer to tell her what rooms the group were staying in. Now she found a trolley of bedding to wheel along and knocked on the first door.

"Who is it?" a female voice wanted to know.

"Service."

A policewoman opened the door. Over her shoulder, Lianne could see Chris, looking rattled.

"I'm sorry," Lianne said. "This room was meant to have been vacated by twelve. I came to…"

"The manager should have been informed that we need it until we're done. Maybe I should call…"

"My mistake," Lianne said. "I'm sorry. Is this the only room you're using?"

"No. Next door as well."

That was the room which Chris and Kerri had been photographed leaving together. Lianne went to the next door, and knocked. Eventually, it opened. Lianne recognized the band's manager, Hud.

"I'm sorry," she said, "did I wake you? Only, the rooms are meant to be empty by…"

"Yeah, yeah…" Hud said. "It's all right. I couldn't sleep. Here…" He thrust a tenner into her hand. "This is for your inconvenience. I don't know when we'll be out. You'd have to ask the police."

Lianne went down a floor. The first room she tried, Fox's, brought no reply. Lianne hesitated. The rest of the band must be in Sapphire's room. Lianne had hoped to get the girl on her own. She couldn't take on three members of Face To Face.

Nevertheless, Lianne couldn't get this close without taking a look. She knocked on the door. Fox opened it. He looked straight at Lianne. It was obvious that he didn't recognize her. Maybe he only saw the uniform.

"Can I help you?" he said.

"I … I'm meant to clean the room," Lianne told him. There were the two girls behind him. Without make-up on, Sapphire looked no older than Lianne, not much prettier, either. If Jem saw her like this, he'd go off her.

"Could you come back later?" Fox said. "We should be gone in an hour or two."

He's nice, Lianne thought, as she reached into her pocket.

"Sure," she said. "But could you do me a favour first? My little sister, she's a big fan of yours. If you could sign something for her…"

Fox frowned and, for a moment, Lianne thought that he was going to say "no".

"How old's your sister?" he asked.

"Twelve," Lianne lied.

"And what about you? Do you like our music?"

"The first single was a bit … mushy," Lianne said. "The new one's good. I like it a lot."

"The rest of the album's more like that," Fox said, almost apologetically. He'd found a piece of hotel notepaper.

"What's your sister's name?"

"Jem. With a 'J'. It's short for Jemima, which she doesn't like." When he was done, Lianne turned to the girls. "Would you mind?"

She leant over Kerri, noticing where Sapphire's handbag was. As she passed the sheet of paper to the bass player, Lianne slipped a little packet into the bag. Then she thanked the band profusely.

"Stay in here as long as you like," she said, with a thin, nervous smile.

There was a hairy moment just afterwards, when she ran into a real chambermaid. Lianne kept her head down and wasn't challenged. She returned to the fourth floor, stood near Chris's room, and waited.

16

"Alan Mackay's car was found abandoned by a canal an hour ago," Hud told the group.

"Was the money in it?" Fox asked.

Hud laughed cynically. "Hardly."

"It makes no sense," Sapphire said. "Why dump the car by a canal but dump the body in the hotel pool?"

Hud had no answer to that.

"By the way, how did you manage to get the money at four in the morning?" Kerri asked Jim.

"Tour receipts," Jim mumbled.

"In *cash*?" Fox queried.

"It's a tax thing," Hud said. "Let's not go into that now, OK? The important thing is sorting out a press statement. I was thinking of something along the lines of: Face To Face deeply regret the death of Alan Mackay, who was a friend of the band. We will do anything we can to assist the police in their enquiries as to how he lost his life. Agreed?"

No one argued.

"We've got permission to leave the hotel," the manager went on. "The police want to interview us again tomorrow, but, for now, let's get to Carlisle, see if we can do the soundcheck before the place is swarming with press."

They headed down to the tour bus. Fox walked with Sapphire. "This is one hell of a day," he said to her.

"I can't believe it," she said. "Someone dying over a silly photograph, to protect our image."

"Maybe it was a coincidence," Fox said, unconvincingly.

"If it wasn't about the photo, it was about the money."

"I guess you're right."

"Excuse me, Sapphire?" It was the female detective from earlier.

"Yes?"

"This'll only take a moment. I didn't get your full name before."

Sapphire gritted her teeth. "Sapphire *is* my full name. I changed it by deed poll."

"Your original name, then."

"I don't tell people that. It's a way of protecting my privacy."

"You'll need to give it to us, I'm afraid," the policewoman said. "I can assure you it won't get out to the press."

Sapphire shook her head. "Look, what's this about? I have an alibi for last night, if you think I'm somehow connected to…"

"Perhaps you wouldn't mind stepping into the manager's office."

Sapphire was annoyed and confused. She looked pleadingly at Fox. "Can he come with me? Will you?"

Fox took her arm.

"I want to know what this is about," Sapphire told him.

The detective gave a very formal smile. "I'd like somebody from the group with you, yes. Come inside."

The two of them stood awkwardly in the office, next to a rubber plant which had been overwatered. The DC stood by the manager's desk.

"This will only take a moment. It's probably a misunderstanding."

"What?" Sapphire asked, irritated. "Look, we need to get to Carlisle."

"I've had a report from a hotel employee, which I'm afraid I have to take seriously. Would you mind emptying your handbag on the table, please?"

"Pardon?"

"It'll only take a moment."

"Why should I?"

"Look," the DC said. "If you think there's something incriminating in there, you can get yourself a lawyer. But I'm afraid that you can't leave until I've seen what's in your bag."

Sapphire looked at Fox. He shrugged, wondering what they were after.

"Want me to get Hud?" he asked.

"Sod it, no," Sapphire told him. "There's nothing in here."

She poured the contents of the bag on to the desk. She was right, there was nothing unusual: lipstick, lipgloss, eye-liner, a mirror, tissues, house keys, a Walkman with headphones, some scraps of paper with notes on them, a comb, a purse.

"You want to look in the purse?" Sapphire asked.

"I don't think that'll be necessary."

The policewoman was fishing among the scraps of paper, using the reverse side of a pen so that she didn't touch anything. There was one small, carefully folded piece of silver paper.

"What's this?" the DC asked.

"I don't know," Sapphire said. "Looks like a gum wrapper."

"It's yours, then?"

"I suppose so. I must have folded it up absent-mindedly. It's not something I often have: gum, that is."

"Would you mind opening it for me?"

"I guess."

"Don't!" Fox said, alarm bells going off in his

mind. He'd read a scene like this in a book some-where. "Don't get your fingerprints on it."

"Do you mind if I do?" The DC got out plastic gloves and tweezers. As the two young musicians watched in silence, she unfolded the silver wrap. Inside it, as Fox feared, was a small quantity of white powder.

"What is it?" DC Wordsworth asked Sapphire. "Speed? Coke? Heroin?"

"I've no idea," Sapphire said. "I've never seen it before."

The DC rewrapped the packet and put it into an evidence bag. "I'm afraid that I'm going to have to ask you to accompany me to the station," she said. "You do not have to say anything but…"

The rest of the words went unlistened to as Sapphire burst into tears and Fox ran out to the tour bus to find Hud.

17

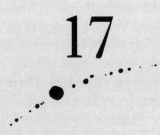

The scene outside the leisure centre was bedlam. This was the smallest gig on the tour and had sold out in a morning. Now there were a hundred journalists clamouring for tickets which couldn't be had. CPM's press office had taken the phone off the hook. Outside the venue, ticket touts kept upping the price of black market tickets. First it was fifty, then sixty, then seventy. By show time, it would top a hundred.

But there might not be a show. Lawyers were busy arranging bail for Sapphire. She had volunteered to take a drugs test which should prove that she didn't use illicit substances. Hud wasn't optimistic about it. Fox could tell the manager wasn't convinced of her innocence. Sapphire was a dark horse. She kept her past very secret. For all Hud knew, she was a former junkie whose history was about to come back and haunt her.

The race was on for the press to find "the truth" about Sapphire. They'd exposed what little there was to tell about Fox, and found nothing on Kerri and Chris. Surprisingly, the police hadn't leaked the details about Alan Mackay. Not yet, anyway.

Sapphire's drugs bust had, at least, taken the heat out of the murder investigation. So far, radio and TV didn't know what to make of that. There was no definite link between Face To Face and Alan Mackay's death. The way the media saw it, American rap artists got mixed up in murder, not British pop groups.

But the media loved exposing artists with drug habits. A bust could mean Sapphire's sacking from the band. Face To Face weren't Oasis or The Rolling Stones. They had a young audience whose parents demanded that they set some kind of example. Also, the American authorities might refuse Sapphire a work permit if she got a drugs conviction. Tonight could be her last performance with the band.

If she ever got there. At seven-thirty, show time, Sapphire still hadn't been released. The support band was, as usual, a local act. Hud told them to extend their set from twenty-five to forty-five minutes.

"But we haven't rehearsed that many songs," one of them complained.

"Then do songs twice, or add extra choruses, guitar solos, whatever. No one's going to be listening to you anyway."

Once the support were on stage, while Kerri was in the bathroom, Chris approached Hud. Fox, pretending to listen to his Walkman, overheard their conversation.

"You've got an understudy for her, haven't you?" Chris asked. "Even if we cancel tonight, we can get Sapphire replaced in a day. It's only sorting out a few bass lines and learning some words, right?"

"It's not that simple," Hud said. "Yes, I originally had an understudy, Yvonne, but then Trudi Garth left The Ghosts and Yvonne got the spot with them. So we'd have to borrow someone from another band."

Fox fumed. He couldn't believe that Chris would be so disloyal as to talk about Sapphire's replacement. To Chris, she was only a cog in a machine. But Fox was a musician, and so was Sapphire. He liked the tender but sinewy sound she got out of her bass guitar. He liked Sapphire's voice: half Trudi Garth, half Dusty Springfield. Losing Art had been bad enough. Losing Sapphire, as far as he was concerned, would mean the end of Face To Face.

The support group's forty-five minutes were up.

"Look," Hud said, "how about if Kerri sings Sapphire's lines as well as her own and we borrow the support's bassist? Could you wing it?"

Kerri shrugged. "My voice is nothing like Sapphire's," she said.

"I'm not going to be part of a substandard show," Fox told him.

"They're going to be screaming like crazy out there," Hud argued. "They'll hardly notice the difference."

"I don't care," Fox said. "No Sapphire, no show."

"I agree," Kerri said, and turned to Chris, who muttered, sheepishly, "Me too."

The leisure centre manager arrived at the dressing-room door.

"It's decision time, Hud. Is tonight's show going to be cancelled?"

"It looks like it," Hud said.

"Then I hope you've got bloody good insurance, because those kids are going to wreck this place!"

Hud's mobile rang. He grunted into it a couple of times, listened, said "Right", then hung up. "They've let her out," he said.

Everybody whooped.

"They agreed for her to take the voluntary drugs test. We'll have the results tomorrow, then we'll see. Right now, she's on her way by helicopter." He turned to the manager. "Make an announcement that the show's going on but there'll be a short delay." He turned to the band. "I'd better go out and meet her, check security. You lot, get ready."

Twenty minutes later, Sapphire was there, looking vulnerable and wasted. Even from the dressing room, Fox could hear the crowd getting impatient, but she took her time getting made up. Fox tried to talk to her.

"Was it really bad?" he asked.

"Humiliating," was all she said.

"Any idea where that wrap came from?"

Sapphire gave her head the smallest of shakes. "It had to be someone close," she whispered.

"Come on," Fox put his arm around her shoulder. "Don't get paranoid. You're talking like it might be one of us."

"Listen," Sapphire said, "no one's going to stop me being angry. But this might be my last gig. I mean to enjoy it."

18

"I've been worried about you," Jem said. "Where've you been?"

"Glasgow," Lianne said. "I saw the gig last night."

"You went without me? All that way? But you don't even like the band!"

"I knew that you couldn't skip work, but I got you something."

Lianne handed over the autographs. Jem was stunned.

"You met them! But how…?"

Lianne grinned. "I hung about near their tour bus. I'm sorry I didn't get Chris. He wasn't with them at the time."

"Who cares? You got Sapphire! She's written my name! Did you tell her who I was?"

"Oh, yes," said Lianne.

"When did you get back from Glasgow?"

"An hour ago."

"Then you won't have heard the news."

"What news?"

"Sapphire's been busted!"

"Never!" Lianne said, feigning incredulity.

"According to Radio One, the band have some kind of morals clause in their contract. She could be sacked after tonight's gig."

"That's awful," Lianne said. "Are you upset?"

"Too right I am. We might have front row seats for the Birmingham gig, but it doesn't mean a thing if Sapphire's not there."

"You poor lamb," Lianne said. "You must be so worried…"

They hugged. "You know," Jem said. "Some girls might get jealous, the way I talk about Sapphire, have her picture all over my walls. But you, you go and get her autograph for me. You're incredible. You know that?"

"If you say so," Lianne replied, modestly. "Only if you say so."

"All right," Hud told Sapphire, in the hotel the following morning. "If the stuff wasn't yours, how did it get into your bag?"

"That's what the police kept asking me, and I kept telling them. I've no idea."

"A fan?" Fox suggested.

"Possibly," Sapphire said. "But they don't usually get near enough to reach into my bag. I don't carry it with me when I sign autographs after a show. Trouble is, for all I know, the wrap could have been in there for days. Who do we know who uses cocaine?"

"Alan Mackay," Hud said.

"You've seen him use it?"

"I've seen the signs: glazed eyes, blocked nose. Charly, or speed, I'd say. It's not unusual – half the industry have been into it at one time or another. Did Alan give it to you?"

"I keep saying," Sapphire insisted, "I don't take drugs."

"We'll soon have the test result to prove it one way or the other."

"And if she's positive?" Fox asked.

"Then she's out."

"If she goes," Fox said, in his most deliberate voice, "I go."

Hud raised his eyebrows to show what he thought of this piece of bravado. Sapphire squeezed Fox's hand.

"There was no need for that, Fox. If I'd been using, I'd deserve to go. But thanks."

Fox smiled sadly at her. He'd never wanted to kiss Sapphire more.

"By the way," Hud said. "Did you tell the police your real name?"

"Had to, didn't I?" Sapphire said.

"And did they ask for proof, *Melanie*?"

"I showed them the same birth certificate I showed you. But they promised not to release the information. I don't want people poring over my past the way they have with Fox."

"Hear, hear," Fox said.

"Got something to hide, have you?" Hud asked, as he left the room.

Sapphire groaned.

"He's in a bad mood today," Fox said.

"He's on the verge of a massive success and thinks I'm about to blow it for him," Sapphire said. "I can understand him being ticked off."

"What's wrong with the name Melanie, anyway?" Fox asked. "Or Mel?"

"No one can use Mel since the Spice Girls. And there was some sappy singer-songwriter in the seventies called Melanie. She did this song about roller-skates. Anyway, maybe I'll change my name again when I leave the band."

"*Leave?*" Fox said. "You're not thinking…"

"Or get thrown out," Sapphire went on.

"That won't happen," Fox said, comfortingly, and put an arm around her waist. "Why was he going on about your birth certificate?"

"Who knows?"

"You faked it, didn't you? You're not really eighteen. And that means…"

Sapphire put a finger to his lips, shushing him. "Ask no questions," she said, "and I'll tell you no lies."

"Sounds fair enough to me," Fox said. He'd often suspected that Sapphire was younger than she said she was. The public only saw Face To Face with make-up on. All four were on show all the time. But first thing in the morning, Sapphire looked nearer sixteen than eighteen. Vulnerable.

Sapphire put her head on his shoulder. After a while, she whispered, "If we weren't in the same band do you think we might…"

She didn't finish the sentence. She didn't have to. It was in her eyes. On her lips. Fox thought carefully. Whatever he said now would remain with him for the rest of his life, he knew that.

"I like to think so," he said, finally. "Do you?"

"Oh, yes," Sapphire said, moving her face closer to his. "I do."

Fox was certain that they were going to kiss, but, before their lips met, the door flew open. It was Hud. This time, he was smiling.

"You're clear!" he told Sapphire. "No finger-prints on the wrap. No illegal substances in your system."

"I told you," Sapphire said.

"I'm sorry I doubted you. But guess who *did* test positive?"

19

FACE TO FACE GIRL CLEARED

Sapphire, eighteen, the singer and bassist from chart-topping group Face To Face has had charges of cocaine possession dropped by Glasgow police after fingerprint and blood tests came up negative. A spokesman said the police accept that cocaine found in her purse was planted on her.

The source of the cocaine is thought to be photographer Alan Mackay, twenty-two, whose body was found floating in Face To Face's hotel swimming pool after he had pestered the band for photo opportunities late on the evening before the bust. Friends say that Mackay spent all his time following the band, and was particularly obsessed with Sapphire. He may have intended the cocaine as a surprise gift. Mackay was ejected from the hotel that night. Blood tests showed that he had ingested large quantities of eighty per cent pure cocaine just before his death. Police speculate that he decided to return to the hotel, concussing himself on the side of the pool when he either fell in or decided to go for a swim.

Pool deaths are notorious in rock music, but Face To Face are the first "teeny-bop" group to attract the dark legends usually ascribed to groups like The Rolling Stones. In an interview on page twelve, guitarist and songwriter Fox discusses the death of their lead singer, their first album, and his desperate desire for the group to be taken seriously.

"Turn to page twelve," Lianne told Jem.

"Hold on," he said. "I haven't finished reading yet. Why have they interviewed Fox? I want to see an interview with Sapphire."

"It's because Fox is the indie type, isn't he? The real musician. That's why he's in here."

"Did you fancy him?" Jem asked.

Lianne wanted him to be jealous, the way she was, but Jem was only teasing. "Not as much as I fancy you, *Jeremy*," she said.

He gave her a playful punch, then they turned to the interview.

FOXPOP. A night on the town with Britain's newest Guitar Hero

Fox is eighteen and wants to be taken seriously. "I've been playing in bands for years. When I was in care, the guitar was the only thing that kept me sane. As soon as I was sixteen, I got out of the home and headed for London. I practised twelve hours a day, playing in a college covers-band for experience. I'm not in this for the money: my idols are Jimi Hendrix and Kurt Cobain. I want respect. But you've got to start some-where. I read about the Face To Face auditions and thought I'd give it a go.

I mean, all right, we're a manufactured band. But we're not The Monkees. We write most of our material, play our own instruments. It's a great experience. I'm only eighteen. Most of my heroes started out playing pop music, then moved on to heavier stuff. So all I'm saying is: Don't look down on me. Give me room to grow."

Hud scrunched up the copy of the *NME* and threw it across the tour bus at Fox. "How dare you?" he said.

"It wasn't supposed to be a formal interview, just a night out," Fox explained. "I asked you if I could talk to the *NME*. You said no, so I left it. The guy knew that what we were saying was off the record."

"But you'd already talked to him," Hud pointed out. "On tape."

"It was meant to be for background."

"Oh, sure. You'd had a few beers and made it clear to this guy that you wanted to be taken seriously. That you're condescending to play pop music until you've got a high enough profile to form a 'serious' band."

"Yeah," Fox said. "Well, so what?"

Hud got up, grabbed the guitarist around the shoulders and started to shake him. "'So *what?*' I'll tell you *what* – this *is* a serious band, far more serious than whatever kind of arty-farty stuff you have in mind. I hand-picked you lot. Face To Face have the potential to be massive, to last for years and years. You could be bigger than ABBA, for Christ's sake!"

Fox broke free of the manager. "I don't like ABBA," he said.

"Then you've got no taste," Hud said, with a grin. "Just remember this: I've got you under contract for five years, and if you walk out of this band before then, I'll take every penny you earn!"

"I'll remember that," Fox said, getting up. He went to the toilet at the back of the bus, the one place where he could block everybody out. At times like this, Fox almost wished that he did take drugs, that he had some way of getting out of himself. But drugs were for losers. He'd serve his five years in the group. He'd make enough money so that he never had to compromise his art again. Also, he decided, he'd save his best songs for himself, not give them to Face To Face. Then, when he went solo, or joined another band, he'd have a treasure chest to dip into. He'd see how Hud liked *that*!

20

Lianne and Jem drove to Birmingham in Jem's dad's car.

"I don't know why you want to get there so early," he said. "After all, there's no point in queuing up. We've already got great seats."

"I want to see the group arrive, don't you?"

"Sort of," Jem said. "But you know what it was like in London, all those thirteen-year-old girls. I'll feel out of place."

"Maybe I can get a picture of you with Sapphire."

"Oh, sure. There's a big chance of that," Jem replied.

"I got the autograph, didn't I? Turn left here."

"But that's not the way to the concert," Jem protested.

"Who said anything about the concert?" Lianne said. "We're going to their hotel."

Jem did as he was told. It was funny. He was two school years older than Lianne, but he always did what his girlfriend told him to do. Except for one thing. She'd met him at a Ghosts concert, the first gig she'd been to. He'd been mad about Trudi Garth then. In fact, afterwards... Lianne didn't want to think about that. She'd always known that she was a substitute. But she hid her jealousy well. Most of the time, anyway. Now and then her mouth moved before her brain had told it what to say. Like now.

"Can I ask you something embarrassing?" Lianne muttered.

"Sure," Jem said.

"When we're ... you know, *fooling around*, do you ever pretend – just to yourself – that I'm Sapphire?"

"Of course not," Jem said, too quickly. "That'd be gross."

Lianne could tell that he was lying. Served her right for asking.

When they got to the hotel, the tour bus wasn't there.

"Are you sure they'll be here?" Jem asked.

"Positive. They'll be doing the soundcheck at the moment. But we'll get to see them when they come back to rest before the show. We need to find a place to..."

"Hey, is that who I think it is?" Jem interrupted

her. He stopped short. "I don't believe it… It … it's *Trudi Garth*!"

He was right. Trudi had dressed down, in denim jacket and jeans. She wore shades. But the unnecessary sunglasses couldn't conceal her from Jem. He got out of the car, leaving the engine running, and ran over to the former Ghosts member. Even as she reached for the camera, Lianne saw red. Jem was meant to be over Garth. Sapphire she could cope with. Sapphire was weak, an enemy who Lianne would be able to overcome. But Trudi Garth was the original enemy, the woman who stole Lianne's boyfriend the very night they met. Lianne had vowed to get her.

Lianne trotted across the tarmac to them. Trudi was signing Jem's jacket.

"Don't mention to anyone that you saw me here, OK?" she was saying to him. "I know I can trust you. I remember you from after our gigs. You're my number one fan, right?"

"Right," Jem said. "Definitely."

"Only I'm having a kind of secret meeting," Trudi explained.

"Enough said," Jem told her. "Only would you mind if my friend here took our photograph? It'd be brilliant to have a photo of the two of us together."

"Sure," Trudi said. "My pleasure."

Lianne got out the camera. She pointed it, but didn't focus. Jem had said *my friend*. Not *my girlfriend*. He hadn't even used her name.

"Here," Trudi said. "Get closer. I'm sure your friend doesn't mind."

She pressed her face against Jem's and opened her mouth, rolling her tongue around in the way that she did on the last Ghosts video, the one that Jem had watched at least a thousand times. Lianne lost control. She dropped the camera and reached into her inside pocket, where the sharpened screwdriver was wrapped in an old sock. It slid out easily.

"Lianne?" Jem said. "What's—"

Then he saw it in her hand. Before Jem could do anything, she was rushing towards them. At first, Jem must have thought it was him she was after. He raised his arms to protect himself, giving Lianne a clear line to Trudi. Lianne held the screwdriver with both hands, raised her arms, then thrust with all her strength, aiming straight at the singer's chest.

That night, in Birmingham, everything came together on stage. The crowd were ecstatic. Fox even improvised a little, improving his solos, adding to them, making Sapphire keep up with him. She seemed to enjoy the challenge. There was nothing wrong with being in Face To Face, he decided. Indeed, there was nothing wrong with trying to be the twenty-first century's ABBA. They'd conquered the UK now. Why couldn't they conquer the world? Next stop, America.

There was one odd thing about the Birmingham

gig, though. It struck Fox throughout the first half of the show, until the crowd got the better of the bouncers, left their places and flooded the front third of the theatre.

The odd thing was this: right in the middle of the front row of their sell-out show, there were two empty seats.

21

"Are you going to show me your passport then?"
Fox asked Sapphire.

"What for?" she asked, sullenly staring out at the clouds floating beneath the aeroplane's window.

"So that I can find out your surname. Oh, come on, you showed it at immigration. I thought we trusted each other."

"Isn't my first name enough?"

"I like *Melanie*. If you're not careful I'll start calling you that."

"Will *not*. Listen, Fox. There are things about me I'd rather people didn't know. Including you. It doesn't mean that I don't care."

"If you say so."

In a huff, Fox put on his headphones and began to read *Music Week*. One article caught his eye.

WHAT'S HAPPENED TO TRUDI GARTH?

Since Trudi Garth quit The Ghosts, her old band have had a number one single and recorded a new album. But what about Trudi? Hardcore Ghosts' fans have been waiting desperately for the promised new product.

At first, there were plenty of rumours: Trudi was recruiting a band. Trudi was on the verge of signing a new deal with Virgin. But then things went quiet. Very quiet.

Trudi has no record company, no agent, no press office. She's left her London flat with no forwarding address or number. Inevitably, unsavoury stories have been circulating. Some of the weirdest ones can be found in the internet discussion group alt.fan.trudi–garth. They include: Trudi has married a joiner from Stevenage and is expecting a baby; Trudi is set to play Madonna in a biopic by Alan Parker; Trudi is hiding in Switzerland, where she's had plastic surgery to cover a horrible facial scar, which she got in a knife attack by a deranged fan; Trudi has found religion and joined a sect called "The Children Of God".

If anyone can confirm any of these stories, please contact the newsdesk.

Fox showed the article to Sapphire.

"You were a fan of hers, weren't you?" Sapphire asked.

"Yeah. Big fan."

"I hate her. But I kind of admire what she's done

– disappearing like that. Maybe I'll do the same thing one day."

"You scare me sometimes," Fox said. "You know that?"

Sapphire smiled and looked out of the window. They were descending into JFK, where press and fans were waiting.

"Shut up and smell the roses," she said.

"Hide that paper from her!"

Lianne's mum put away the tabloid with Face To Face on the cover. It seemed that the group were becoming even more successful in America than they were at home.

"It's all right," Lianne's father told Jem. "The doctor said he'd come and have a word before we visit Lianne."

Jem nodded but said nothing. He was beginning to blame both parents for Lianne's condition. She was their only child. It looked like they'd spoiled her from the start, giving in to Lianne's every whim and, later, her every tantrum. Both worked hard: her mother was a top lawyer while her father owned a PR firm which did a lot of work for the government. They made bundles of money. Lianne was never short of anything, except for their time.

"I wondered," the doctor said, when he arrived, "whether I might have a word with Jeremy alone."

Reluctantly, Lianne's parents went back to the waiting room.

110

"How is she?" Jem asked.

"We have a lot of work to do before she's better."

"And what happens then? Do they charge her with grievous bodily harm?"

"Not unless Ms Garth insists. Lianne's parents seem to have a lot of pull with the police."

"You're telling me," Jem said. "Do you know that, before I met her, Lianne tried to burn her school down because a teacher gave her a detention she thought was unfair? Or that her first boyfriend's parents took out a court order to stop Lianne from stalking him after he'd dumped her?"

"Those details are in her records," the doctor said. "And a lot more besides. What I want to do now is establish exactly what happened in your relationship with Lianne."

Jem told the story from the start. "I met her at a Ghosts gig. The place had unreserved seating, so you had to get there early if you wanted a place near the front. I was there four hours before it started. So was Lianne. We got talking in the queue."

"Who talked first – you or her?"

"She picked me up – no question of that. I'm pretty shy around girls, but I was obsessed with Trudi Garth – I had her name written out in studs on the back of my denim jacket. So Lianne started talking to me about Trudi. By the time we'd got in, we were friends."

"Just friends?"

"Sure. No kissing, or anything like that. I thought that she was a bit young for me, but it was good to have company. I felt out of place. The Ghosts were moving from being a rock band to being a pop group. The audience was changing, too. At seventeen, I was the oldest person in the front half of the hall. Lots of the kids there were younger than Lianne.

"Anyway, we enjoyed the show and, afterwards, we exchanged phone numbers. I kissed her good night – it was a bit more than a peck, I suppose, but not a big deal. Then I went to wait at the stage door. I always did that at Ghosts gigs, meeting the band, getting autographs. Lianne couldn't stay. Her dad was picking her up, or so she said.

"The band took ages to come out. By the time they did, there were only a few of us left. It was raining. Trudi Garth recognized me and gave me a little hug and a kiss on the cheek. Then she offered me and the other fans a lift to the station in the tour bus, because we were in danger of missing the last train. It was brilliant."

The doctor made some more notes. "But Lianne hadn't left, had she?"

Jem shook his head. "She was watching. She saw me next to Trudi on the bus. I didn't know about it until the day she attacked Trudi with the screwdriver. She was yelling *'You stole me boyfriend!'* But nothing happened and, anyway, I wasn't even Lianne's boyfriend then.

"A couple of weeks after that gig I called her and asked if she fancied going to the *Smash Hits* concert. I told her about how I'd met Trudi. She said she'd go, and invited me round for a meal because her parents would want to meet me before they allowed her to go all the way to Birmingham with me.

"We got on fine at the meal the night before. Lianne cooked and we sort of agreed to go out with each other. I remember making a joke about 'as long as you don't mind me being mad about Trudi Garth'. She laughed. The next day, I came down with food poisoning. Lianne went to the gig alone."

"And you didn't see Trudi Garth again until Lianne attacked her at that car park in Birmingham?"

"No," Jem explained. "Trudi left The Ghosts and disappeared. Lianne and I got interested in Face To Face, so they kind of … took over."

"And you became obsessed with the singer called Sapphire?"

"No," Jem insisted. "Lianne kept going on about who did I fancy the most and I said Sapphire because it was true, but it was only for something to say. Lianne was my girlfriend. I'd grown out of having crushes on unattainable women."

"Until you saw Trudi Garth in the car park."

"I only wanted to say hello," Jem protested.

"And you didn't know about the screwdriver attacks or the crank calls that Lianne had made to Sapphire?"

"No," Jem insisted. "I'd've reported her. But I'd

never seen Lianne get violent, or mad, not until that afternoon in Birmingham."

The doctor nodded, and finished making his notes. "She wants to see you," he said, "but not her parents, who she blames for neglecting her. I'll take you in."

"You won't leave me alone with her?" Jem asked, nervously.

"Don't worry, she's restrained. But be prepared for her to look very different."

22

The Biggest British Band since The Beatles said the cover of *Rolling Stone*. The interview inside the magazine gave Face To Face far more respect than they got from the serious music press in the UK. Sapphire watched Fox preening himself as he read it. He liked being treated like a serious musician.

The balance of power in the band was changing. Although the interview was meant to be with all of them together, most of the quotes used were from Fox and Sapphire. Especially Sapphire.

The story of Sapphire being set up for a drugs bust and the murder of Alan Mackay was given lots of space. The journalist was impressed with Sapphire's mysterious past. Then there were Annie Leibowitz's photos of Sapphire on her own, wearing less make-up than usual, dressed only in a long T-shirt, writing a song on the beat-up acoustic guitar she'd brought along to the first ever Face To Face audition.

The interview came out on the day they flew home, first class, after three weeks on tour. Every day in America had been mad, with fans following them everywhere, from little kids to grown men. It wasn't just young teenagers who liked them. The college audience had adopted them, too. Huge crowds waited outside all their sold-out shows.

The first week they'd arrived, *Face To Face* had rocketed to number one in the US singles chart, and it was still there. Next time the band played America, they'd have to perform in sports arenas.

Hud was complaining about something. Sapphire snapped out of her thoughts and gave him her attention.

"What were you thinking of when you told them this? You stupid girl! It's completely off-message."

"What are you talking about?" Sapphire asked.

Hud read out the offending passage. "*Sapphire loves songwriting. 'We had a lot of help with the songs that are on our first album,' she said, after giving me a preview of a new song she's written alone, on acoustic guitar. 'For the next album, I want to write all my songs completely by myself, but they'll only get on if they're good enough.'*"

"What's wrong with that?" Sapphire asked. "It's true."

"I'll tell you what's wrong," Hud said. "The rest

of us have been telling the world that we brought in other songwriters to smooth out the edges of your own songs, not to write them in the first place. The fans are meant to believe that you wrote every song yourselves."

"But it's a lie!" Sapphire said.

"I don't care if it's a lie! This is public relations. We're selling product. And you're product, too."

Sapphire swore at him.

"Go on then," Hud said. "Get too big for your boots. Pretend you're Joni Mitchell. But I warn you, get out of line again and you're gone. Nobody in this band is irreplaceable."

Sapphire looked at the others. Fox gave her a sympathetic smile. Chris and Kerri conspicuously turned away and stared out of the window.

They were about to land. Sapphire checked that she had her passport, then caught Fox glancing over her shoulder at it. He was still trying to find out her real surname.

"You won't need that," he said. "They'll be taking us in the VIP way."

"I don't believe it!" Kerri called. "Come and look at this!"

They were descending into Heathrow. Fox, Sapphire and Hud went over to the window, ignoring the "Fasten seatbelts" sign. The airport was awash with people. In America there'd been a thousand fans waiting to see them arrive and three times that number watching them go. But beneath them now were countless people, over five thousand come to welcome them home.

"This is it," Hud said. "We've made it. Remember this for the rest of your lives. No one can take this away from us. You're the biggest band in the world!"

Lianne looked painfully thin. The white-cotton gown was tied loosely over the restraints which held her to the bed. The paleness of her face took years off her age. Jem could hardly believe that she was the same girl he'd been going out with for nine months.

"Thanks for coming," she said.

Her voice was a little slurred. The drugs, he thought.

"I've missed you," he said, honestly.

"Me too," she told him. "Please hold my hand." He didn't know what to say, but took her hand and squeezed.

"The doctor tells me you're going to get better," he said, "but it might take a while."

"I don't want to get better. They'll only put me in prison."

"That won't happen. Not unless Trudi Garth presses charges, which is unlikely. She knows that you're very ill. You weren't responsible for…"

"Say it," Lianne interrupted. "*Mentally* ill."

"You'll get better," Jem assured her.

"That's right," Lianne said, a new, cynical tone in her voice that Jem hadn't heard before. "They can fix my head, but Trudi'll never be able to wear a bikini or pose naked on an album cover again."

"That's not funny," Jem said. "I don't like you when you're like this."

A tiny tear trickled down Lianne's cheek. "I'm sorry," she said. "Help me."

"I'll do whatever I can," Jem said, reaching forward to hold her.

"Lean closer."

Jem did. He thought that she wanted to kiss him, but, instead, she whispered in his ear. "Have you got your penknife on you?"

"I … uh." Jem didn't know how to respond. He backed away.

"Cut me out of this," Lianne insisted. "We can get away from here."

"You're mad," Jem said, not thinking what he was saying.

"Of course I am," Lianne told him. "I always have been. That's why you're mad about me. We'll run away together. I've got plenty of money stashed. Come on, do it now, while the doctor's talking to my mum and dad. I know another way out. Come on, Jem. You've always done what I asked you to. Don't back out on me now. Come on, Jem. Jem?"

Jem didn't hear any more, because he'd left the hospital room.

23

Hud lined up two showcase gigs to end the year: Wembley Arena, followed by a Royal Variety Show appearance. Fox complained about the latter.

"If it was good enough for The Beatles, it's good enough for us," Hud argued. Their album had gone straight into the chart at number one, and remained there. Their third single, *The Spirit Lives*, had entered the chart at number one, to nobody's surprise, and was likely to stay there over Christmas. If their fourth single got to number one, they would get a place in the record books, second only to The Spice Girls. But it was a big if. Groups never stayed this big for long, Hud warned. They had to milk their success while they were at the top.

Face To Face appeared on soft drinks cans and had

their own brand of designer jeans in the shops for Christmas. Sapphire and Kerri appeared on TV promoting a brand of chewing gum. Chris did a commercial for men's body cologne. Only Fox refused to do any endorsements or TV ads. When Sapphire asked him why, he said something about not wanting to prostitute his music. Sapphire said he was mad. It was easy money.

"Where are you going for Christmas?" he had asked her, the week before. He'd assumed that they'd stay in the house, like last year, but Chris and Kerri had just announced that they were visiting the Caribbean. Separately, of course.

"I've got these friends…" she muttered.

"I'll be in the house alone, then," Fox moaned. Hud was also going to be abroad.

"Sorry," Sapphire said. "I can't take you with me."

"S'OK. Just seems funny. Here I am in the most successful band in the world, and I have to spend Christmas by myself."

"Go to any nightclub on Christmas Eve," Sapphire advised, in a gentle voice. "You won't have to go home alone, I guarantee."

"That's not what I'm after."

She put down the guitar she'd been strumming and looked him straight in the eye. "What are you after then?"

He went over and put an arm around her waist. "Chris and Kerri have been getting away with it for months, Sapphire. Maybe it's time for us."

She shook her head with more force than seemed necessary. "No," she said. "The time's gone."

"What do you mean?" Fox asked, confused. All these months, they'd been crazy for each other, making hints, giving whispered encouragement. Now he was telling her that the time was right. They could be together.

"I want a guy who'll walk through fire for me," Sapphire said, not looking at him as she spoke. "A guy who'll risk anything. You're saying that we might as well have a fling because Hud will let us get away with it. No thanks."

"I didn't say a *fling*!" Fox protested.

"That's all we could have," Sapphire explained. "We're mates now. We've shared tiny dressing rooms, seen each other at our best and worst. There's none of the mystery you need for romance. Six months ago, I was interested in you. But I'm not any more. Sorry."

"I don't know what to say." He'd blown it, Fox realized. He'd always thought of their relationship as being in the future. But their future was in the past.

"Do us all a favour," Sapphire said. "Write a song about it. That's what songwriters do, isn't it? They convert their misery into gold dust. We need a fourth number one. We need a second album. Go write."

"Maybe we could write together," Fox suggested.

"I don't think so," Sapphire said.

She reached over and squeezed his hand affectionately. She had too much black eye-liner on, Fox noticed. Or maybe it was smudging because she was starting to cry. Whatever. Before he could say anything else she put down her guitar and left the room, muttering something about seeing Hud before he went on holiday.

Fox didn't see her again that year. But he followed her advice. He spent Christmas writing sad songs, resentful songs, some about Sapphire, some about forbidden love. He made sure that the lyrics were obscure enough to be universal, but clear enough for Sapphire to know what he meant.

He didn't know where she'd gone, though. The others were away. Jim, now the chief of security, said he didn't know where Sapphire had got to, either.

"Has she not taken a bodyguard with her?" Fox asked.

"Not unless she hired one herself."

That was odd – Fox's bodyguard accompanied him everywhere, including the clubs where he went on Boxing Day. It was the first time he'd been out alone since the group's third number one. Everywhere he went, he was mobbed. There was no chance of his having a conversation with anyone, never mind finding female company. By midnight, he was in the band's rehearsal studio, writing bitter songs about the shallowness of success. By four in the morning, he was singing exactly what he felt.

* * *

On the day that Chris, Kerri and Hud were due to fly back from their respective holidays, Sapphire still hadn't reappeared. Fox rang Jim again.

"She's not absent without leave," the security chief explained. "She's on holiday, as far as I'm concerned. You're due in the studio Monday to work on the new album. If she doesn't turn up, that's when we have a problem."

Fox remembered that Jim had a bit of a thing about Sapphire. According to Sapphire, he'd put the moves on her more than once.

"Are you sure she's not with you?" he asked.

"I should be so lucky," Jim said, sarcastically. "She's probably on a beach somewhere. Which is where you should have been."

Fox listened back to the songs he'd written over the previous two weeks. He transferred most of them on to a tape which he would put into his safety-deposit box. They were songs that he was saving for his solo career. Then he re-recorded the ones which he thought would work for Face To Face, the more poppy ones. Finally, he went to work on the big ballad, the song he'd written about Sapphire at four in the morning, the one he wanted as their fourth single. It was called: *Too Little, Too Late*.

Time to stop telling lies
I know it's over now
It's time to dry my eyes
Thought we'd make it somehow

Had my head in the sand
But I thought we had to wait
Should have tipped my hand
I gave too little, too late

You tried so many times
To get through to me
Thought we had the time
I was too blind to see

You always wanted me
But I kept closing the gate
Said I loved being free
What I really meant was hate
You said be what you wanna be
I said too little, too late

The demo was rough in places, partly because Fox was singing and crying at the same time, but mainly because some sections of the song weren't suited to his vocal range. Fox thought the song would lend itself perfectly to a four part harmony, with he and Sapphire taking the lead vocals. Maybe, when she sang it with him, she'd realize that the words were from the heart. Maybe she'd change her mind.

But Sapphire didn't show up for the songwriting session on the Monday. Nor did she show up on Tuesday. Nobody knew where she was.

24

"She's in breach of contract," Hud said. "If she doesn't get here by the end of the week, she's history."

"I'll find her," Fox promised. "But haven't you any idea where she's gone – a family address, a friend, something…?"

"If I had, don't you think I would have looked there?"

"The last time I spoke to her, she said she was going to see you."

"I didn't see her after that," Hud said. "She phoned me on Christmas Eve, told me she was taking off to see friends. She said something about doing some thinking. I told her to think of some new songs. That's all."

"I'm going to look for her," Fox insisted, "but I need more to go on."

Hud shrugged. "I can tell you her surname, if you think that'll help."

"I already know it."

"She told you?"

"No, I saw it on her passport. Duckenfield."

"That's right. Not that common a name. Wouldn't be hard to find her – if she's using it, which she won't be."

"Are you sure you haven't got an address?"

"The address on her contract is the same as the one on yours – the band house. Look, Fox, if she doesn't show up, I'll hire a detective. But it wouldn't surprise me if she's done a runner. Checked your bank account recently?"

"No." Fox didn't read his statements. Hud gave the group cash when they needed it. Royalties and performance fees were paid direct into each band member's bank account. An independent accountant checked that each band member received all that they were due.

"Well, you'll find an awful lot of money there. And Sapphire earned more than you – an extra two hundred grand from the gum advert alone. That amount of money can go to a girl's head."

"Sapphire's not like that," Fox protested.

"Who knows what Sapphire's really like?" Hud said. "She's a mystery. Want to tell me something? How come with her picture in the paper all the time, nobody's come forward to say that they knew Sapphire before she was a star?"

"She's changed her image," Fox said. "So what?"

"If she can lose one life so easily, she can lose another."

"But suppose something's happened to her? All those crank calls … the screwdriver girl…"

"That's something I forgot to tell you," Hud said. "They caught the screwdriver girl."

Fox was confused. "I didn't see it in the papers."

"It was hushed up. She's in a mental institution."

"I see," Fox said. "Well, I suppose she didn't actually hurt anybody."

Hud didn't reply. "Got some songs to play me?" he asked, after a while.

Fox got out the demos. He played Hud three songs. The manager seemed fairly impressed.

"We can do something with those," he said. "A couple of album tracks and a B-side. But you're a singles group. I need to get you a fourth number one."

"I've written it," Fox said. "You're going to love it. But I want to work it up with the others first. It really needs Sapphire's voice."

Hud put a hand on Fox's shoulder, an unusually paternal gesture. "I know how you feel about Sapphire, Fox. But don't count on her coming back. We might be looking for a replacement."

Why did he seem so pessimistic? Fox wondered. She's only been gone a fortnight.

But the fortnight stretched to the end of the week. The band began recording without her. Fox began ringing all of the Duckenfields in the phone book. The only "Melanie" he found was four years old.

Another week passed. Hud seemed reluctant to replace Sapphire. In America, especially, she was the biggest star in the group. But rumours were starting to spread on the internet. Journalists kept calling and the press office kept stonewalling them. The band couldn't keep Sapphire's disappearance a secret for ever.

"I thought you were going to hire a detective," Fox said, at the end of the first week's recording sessions. He'd been recording Sapphire's bass parts for her, but couldn't get the sound right.

"I did," Hud said. "I'd've told you if he found anything."

"He found *nothing at all*?"

"Sapphire made a big cash withdrawal from her bank account on Christmas Eve. Her money's not been touched since. She's vanished, Fox. She's disappeared to wherever she came from. And I don't think she's coming back."

25

The recording sessions continued. Fox considered leaving the band. With Sapphire gone, it wasn't the same. Chris and Kerri were openly sharing a room now. Fox was the odd man out. But if he broke his contract, he could be sued. His royalties would be suspended, as Sapphire's had been.

Now and then a terrible suspicion crossed his mind. Something had happened to her. Hud refused to tell the police that she was missing. He said that, if he did, it'd be all over the press the next day. There would be suicide stories, fan hysteria. It could be the end of the group. No, he argued, wait until they were sure Sapphire had left, then replace her.

But when would they be sure? If she was alive and

well, how could she be so cruel as not to call him? Fox remembered what had happened to Alan Mackay. The police had never determined whether his death was an accident or murder. It was mid-January and the country was frozen. Suppose that Sapphire's body was under a blanket of ice somewhere?

The recording sessions weren't going well. Fox's new songs were received without enthusiasm. Chris and Kerri were going in a softer direction than Fox was comfortable with. Without Sapphire, nothing gelled. They were on the verge of taking a break when Hud called a band meeting.

"Sapphire phoned me last night," he said.

Everyone perked up.

"And?" Fox was the first to say.

"She's not coming back."

"Why?" Kerri asked. "What more did she say?"

"Not a lot," Hud told them. "She mumbled something about pressure and not caring about the money, then she hung up."

"Where was she calling from?" Fox asked.

"She withheld the number."

Fox thought the manager must be lying. Sapphire hadn't called. It was the way that Hud was withholding eye contact which gave him away. But Fox couldn't challenge him. It was only an intuition. Maybe he was getting paranoid.

"What else did she say?" Chris asked.

"Nothing. That was the whole call. I didn't get the chance to ask her anything before she hung up."

They sat in silence for a while. It was Kerri who finally asked the crucial question. "What do we do now?"

"We replace her," Hud said.

"Got an understudy lined up?" Fox asked, suspiciously.

"Not exactly," Hud said. "But I've got someone in mind. You'd have to want her. I'm not going to impose anyone against your wishes."

That hadn't stopped him from bringing in Chris, Fox thought. But they'd been younger then, less successful, more easily controlled.

"Who?" Kerri asked.

"I'll bring her over tomorrow. Best if you meet her in person rather than go on reputation. Now, I want to talk about press strategy."

Hud's strategy was simple. They needed something to distract the press from the significance of Sapphire's leaving.

"We put out two announcements on the same day," he said. "By mutual agreement, Sapphire has left the group to start a solo career."

"Did she say that?" Kerri asked.

"No, but the truth's irrelevant. Then we top that by admitting that the rumours in the tabloids are true. Chris and Kerri are in love."

The couple looked at each other. Neither seemed too enthusiastic to share their happiness with the whole world.

"I thought that having a couple in the band would upset our fan base," Chris pointed out. "You nearly threw us out. Why the change of mind?"

"It's all I could think of," Hud admitted. "We'll give a press conference, announce that we're auditioning for Sapphire's replacement. Then, before the press can get their teeth into that, we'll drop the bombshell."

"What bombshell?" Kerri asked.

"That you two are engaged to be married."

There was a long jaw-dropping silence. "I'm only nineteen," Kerri said, finally. "I'm too young to get married."

"I didn't say you had to go through with it," Hud told them. "In fact, we'll milk your breaking off the engagement for all it's worth. But that's at least six months away."

"I'm not sure about this," Chris argued. "It's like our whole lives are being arranged to make good publicity."

"Wakey, wakey!" Hud said. "What do you think's been going on for the last year? We live and die by publicity. Now, will you go along with it?"

Chris and Kerri looked at each other. Fox was disgusted with them. He was disgusted with himself for not saying anything. Chris turned to Hud. "You're paying for the ring," he said.

"Deal!" Hud said.

Fox stomped out of the room. Maybe he should go to the police. Sapphire was the second singer connected with Hud to have vanished from view. It was hard to believe Hud capable of hurting people, though. The manager seemed so amenable, so infectiously ambitious. But he had an authoritarian side, as the band well knew.

Suppose that Sapphire had gone to see Hud, like she'd told Fox that she was going to the last time he saw her? Suppose she and Hud had had a row? Suppose the manager got carried away?

Fox had to find Sapphire. He had to find out the truth.

26

The press conference went according to plan. Nearly all the questions were aimed at Kerri and Chris. As expected, news of their engagement kept Sapphire's absence off the front pages. There was some speculation about why the singer hadn't given a press conference herself, the way Trudi Garth did when she was leaving The Ghosts. But the journalists seemed to accept Hud's version of events. Sapphire's solo career would, they presumed, be news on another day.

Afterwards, Jim drove the four of them back to the house. Kerri was excited by her new engagement ring. Chris seemed oddly quiet. Fox hid behind a copy of *Mojo* magazine. The traffic was slow, due to the icy conditions. At one point, a couple of girls at a bus stop spotted the band. They ran over and banged on the side of the car, asking for autographs. Fox wanted to wind down the window. Hud wouldn't let him. "You never know what's out there," was all he said.

Fox gave an exaggerated shrug and blew the girls a kiss as they drove away. He couldn't even meet the fans any more. What good was fame when all it did was further isolate you from people?

That evening, the group were getting together in the rehearsal room. They had more studio time booked for next week, but had already recorded the only new material they had. None of the band were blown away by it. Fox hadn't shown anybody *Too Little, Too Late* yet. He'd been waiting for Sapphire to return.

Fox got to the room before the others. Maybe he'd got the time wrong. The rehearsal room was a dark, soundproofed basement. At this time of year, the large space was very cold. Oil radiators barely took the chill out of the air. Fox plugged in his guitar and began to play, humming the tune of *Too Little, Too Late*, trying to figure out what kind of arrangement the song needed. A lot depended on whether the new singer could match Sapphire's vocal range. A lot depended on the new singer, full stop.

As Fox went through the song a second time, something funny happened. He could swear that somebody was playing along with him. He stopped and there was no sound, or only the echo of sound. It was hard to tell. He looked around, but the room was full of shadows. He could see no one.

Fox began to play again. This time, the bass was louder, almost muscular. The sound could be Sapphire's, only it was stronger, like she'd been practising constantly while she'd been away. Fox stopped mid-verse and the bass continued for a couple of notes before dying.

He nearly said her name, but she spoke first. Her voice was familiar. "That's a terrific song. Are you saving it for yourself or giving it to the group?"

"It's for the group," Fox said.

"I'd love to sing it with you."

"Thanks," Fox said, as the woman stepped out of the shadows. "I'm honoured."

"I've been waiting for you," she said. "I asked Hud to tell you an earlier time than the others, so that I'd get you on your own first. It was you I wanted to see, not the other two. You're the real talent in this band. Believe me, I'd kill to work with you."

She held out her hand. Fox hesitated. He felt like he'd be betraying Sapphire. But he couldn't refuse. Not her. Fox smiled shyly, then shook hands with Trudi Garth.

27

Fox and Trudi were playing together when Chris and Kerri came down to the meeting.

"What's going on here?" Chris asked, recognizing the former Ghosts member immediately.

"Looks like an audition to me," Hud said.

"But *her*?" Kerri asked. "Of all people!"

Fox stopped playing. "Don't say no before you've given this a chance," he told the others. "It might just work."

Kerri turned to Trudi. "You called us a manufactured group," she said.

"So what?" Trudi said, in a tone which was amused rather than mocking. "It's true, isn't it?"

"You had a go at us for not writing our own songs," Chris pointed out.

"Looks like I had the right effect," Trudi said. "Fox has just written a really good one."

Hud turned on a couple more lights and, for the first time, Fox got a good look at Trudi. She was at least five years older than him, but looked timeless: a tall blonde with huge eyes and a body that belonged in a swimsuit. She wasn't a classic beauty, like Sapphire. Trudi's nose was a little snub, her jaw a bit too square. She looked tough. She looked rock 'n' roll.

"What's with the jeans and sweater?" Kerri asked her. "Trying to soften your image?"

"I've become a vegetarian," Trudi said, and laughed.

"I thought you were going solo," Chris said.

"I changed my mind," Trudi told them. "I work best in a band."

"Why don't we play a song?" Fox suggested. "Trudi's been listening to the album. She's learnt most of our set."

Reluctantly, the others took their places behind the instruments. Kerri played a drum roll and Trudi came in behind Chris's organ, her timing perfect. When Trudi sang *hard, but sweet*, it felt right to Fox. The words summed her up better than they did Sapphire. When they sang the chorus – *I need a lover, Can take the pace, Got to meet you, Face to face* – Fox found himself looking at Trudi, listening to her voice alone. This was a woman whose picture used to be all over his bedroom wall. Later she was plastered across his locker in the children's home. He'd dreamt about Trudi when he went to sleep, the tips of his fingers still raw from guitar practice. Now she was singing opposite him.

"Well?" Trudi asked, when they'd finished. "Have you heard enough?"

"I have," Fox said.

"Chris?" Hud asked.

He looked at Kerri, but her face was concealed behind the drum kit. "It sounded fine to me," he said, somewhat hesitantly.

Kerri got up and walked over to Trudi, until they were standing face to face, not speaking. Trudi was four inches taller than Kerri, two inches taller than Sapphire. Kerri had felt outshone by Sapphire, Fox realized. Maybe she'd been looking forward to being in the limelight more. With Trudi in the band, upfront, and her behind the drums, Kerri would always be overshadowed.

Kerri turned to Hud. "Trudi's too old," she said.

"Maybe she'll broaden the group's appeal," the manager pointed out.

"I didn't know we were short of fans," Kerri riposted.

Trudi whispered something to Kerri which Fox couldn't hear. Kerri flinched. Fox glanced at Chris, who was looking increasingly uncomfortable. "We need her," he said. Chris, to his surprise, nodded agreement.

"That's it, then," Kerri said. "I'm outvoted."

"I want it to be unanimous," Hud told her.

"So do I," Trudi said. "I want us to be friends."

"Oh yeah," Kerri said, "like you really care about anyone, Trudi Garth. I've watched you on tour. You're a hard bitch. I'll bet you can't stand anyone being more successful than you!"

Trudi slapped Kerri across the face and the drummer burst into tears.

"On second thoughts, maybe we can do without a unanimous vote," Hud said. "A little tension in a band's good for creativity, or so they say. Now, Fox, I believe you've got a new song for us?"

28

The news that Trudi Garth had replaced Sapphire made the front pages, not just in the music press and the tabloids, but in the broadsheets, too. It created controversy among the group's fans, who were divided fifty-fifty over whether it was a good idea. Still there was no word about Sapphire. The band's publicity office was overwhelmed with enquiries about interviews. Everybody was told the band were too busy recording.

A release date was set for *Too Little, Too Late*. Hud wanted to time it very carefully, making sure that the single went straight in at number one. They didn't want to be up against some novelty hit, or a charity record. Face To Face wanted to go down in history for entering the charts at number one with their first four singles.

In the studio there were tensions. Trudi had brought lots of material with her. Some of it seemed more suitable for The Ghosts than for Face To Face, unless they changed direction. That wasn't all. Trudi wrote her songs on her own. In the past, everyone had chipped in on songs, suggesting ideas – lyrics, guitar riffs, a new middle eight, whatever – until they were sure that they'd got it right. Trudi was having none of that.

Until Trudi arrived, the group had shared their publishing royalties four ways, regardless of who first had the idea. If there was an outside songwriter involved, he or she would get a fifth share. When they started, Hud had explained that this was the best way to avoid rows. Lennon/McCartney didn't argue over who contributed how much. Neither should they.

Trudi argued that, if she wrote a song herself, she should keep all the publishing royalties.

"Look," Trudi said to Fox, as they completed mixing the orchestral overdubs on *Too Little, Too Late*, "this song is going to be a massive worldwide hit. It's going to sell millions and millions of copies. Lots of people are going to cover it. You could make enough money to retire on from this song alone. Why give three-quarters of that away?"

It was a compelling argument, but Fox wasn't having it.

"I'm not doing this for the money," he said.

"If you aren't now, you will be eventually," Trudi

143

argued. "Success like this doesn't last for ever. Make a stupid financial decision now and it'll haunt you for the rest of your life. All right, so you all mixed it up for the first album. You were young then. But you're a professional now. Take advice from another professional."

Fox said he'd think about it.

Trudi made it clear from the start that she wouldn't live in the band house. *I'm too old to be a member of The Monkees* was all she said by way of explanation. She returned to her penthouse flat after rehearsals. Fox was disappointed. He wanted to get to know her better, to build up the kind of rapport he'd had with Sapphire, maybe even something more than that. Chris and Kerri, however, were relieved.

"It feels like she's a session musician," Kerri said, after Trudi had gone home for the day, "leeching on our success."

"She's got some good song ideas," Fox tried to argue.

"They sound like Ghosts' rejects to me," Chris reckoned. "If we don't sound like ourselves, we're finished."

He and Kerri went upstairs. "We're ordering a take-away," Chris told Fox. "Want some?"

"No, I'm off out."

Chris didn't ask where he was going. They'd been in each other's pockets all day. Each of them needed time to themselves. Soon, they would be on tour again, stuck inside their bubble of fame, competing for the same air.

Fox phoned for a taxi. When it arrived, he ran outside and jumped in, avoiding the fans who clustered around the steps outside the house. Sometimes he didn't have the patience to deal with them. It was time, he thought, to get a place of his own, a protected penthouse like Trudi Garth's. Or, he should say, like he imagined Trudi's place to be, for she'd never invited him to her home.

Fox and Trudi had an odd relationship. They'd written a couple of songs together. She flirted with him, or, at least, he thought that she did. At other times, she acted like she was his big sister. Trudi must realize how much he fancied her. If so, she'd done nothing about it.

Maybe it was the age difference. Trudi claimed to be twenty-four. For that to be true, she'd have to have made her first single when she was sixteen. Kerri reckoned the singer was nearer thirty. Fox didn't care. Age was only a number, as far as he was concerned. He hoped that he and Trudi would become closer when they went out on tour.

But it wasn't Trudi who was on Fox's mind as he asked the taxi driver to drop him off on a busy corner. He tucked his long hair under a woolly hat and stepped out into the busy Soho streets. Then he walked briskly to the *Coach and Horses*.

"Sure you're over eighteen, son?"

"You can see my driving licence, if you like," Fox replied, in a deep voice. He hadn't been asked his age in a while, but at least it meant that the landlord hadn't recognized him. He bought a pint and sat down in a shabby corner away from the TV, which was showing football. No one paid any attention to him.

The man Fox was after came in ten minutes later. He had black, heavy-rimmed glasses and wore a black leather coat, not quite full length, with an old-fashioned cut, beneath which Fox could make out a white polo-neck. When the man went to the bar, Fox could see the dandruff which had flaked from his thinning dark hair. Then the man turned and, seeing Fox, smiled. He had a horrible smile: fat-faced and creepy. But Fox had been told that this was the one man who could help him. The Hunter.

"Take that hat off," Hunter said, in a Yorkshire accent which didn't fit his face. "You look like a stupid bugger. I'm surprised they served you."

Fox took the hat off and pushed his hair behind his ears. He felt conspicuous, exposed like this, but he was the only person under forty in the pub. He wasn't going to be hassled by fans, not here.

"Brought the money?"

Fox got out the envelope. "Two grand. Used tens."

The man slipped it into his jacket without counting the cash.

146

"And who is it we're after? Family?"

"No," Fox said. "A girl. A famous girl."

"How old?"

"I'm not sure. She might have lied about her age, but her passport said she was eighteen."

"Passports are easy to fix, if you've got money."

"She certainly had money. I mean … *has*. She might only be seventeen. Or younger, even. Not older than eighteen."

"Name?"

"The name on her passport was Melanie Duckenfield. The name she was using was one word: Sapphire."

"Last seen?"

Fox told him. He went through everything he knew about Sapphire, provided private photos where, without make-up, she looked her age, whatever that was.

"All right," the Hunter said, after half an hour, "down to the nitty-gritty. Why's she gone missing?"

"I wish I knew," Fox said.

"You see, there's missing and *missing*. If she doesn't want to be found, that won't stop me finding her. But if someone else doesn't want her found – if *something's happened* to her, I can't guarantee results."

"But you might find out who's responsible?"

"More than might," Hunter said, with a confident, creepy smile.

"Find out," Fox said. "Whatever the cost." He

gave the man his mobile number, told him the best times to ring.

"I'll call once a week," Hunter said, "for as long as you pay money into this account. When I find anything definite, I'll call straight away. I take it that if she wants to be invisible, you want me to keep it that way, just let you know where she is?"

"That's right," Fox said. "What's even more important is that the press don't find out where she is, because, you know…"

Hunter leant forward and gripped Fox's wrist so tightly that it hurt. "If I sell a story to the press, I sell my self-respect and I lose all my professional credibility. Got that? They might find out she's missing, but it won't be from me."

"I believe you," Fox said, and Hunter released his wrist, drained his drink, and was gone. Fox looked around. Suddenly he was aware that everybody in the seedy pub was carefully ignoring him. Fox changed his mind about phoning for a taxi and hurried out into the street.

Fox walked for a few minutes, but then a wind got up. As he looked for a taxi, it started to rain. Fox realized that he'd left his hat behind. Too late to think about that now. But he'd been walking through central London, undisguised, a member of the most famous pop group in the world. Not one person had approached him, or pointed. How could that be?

"Hey, Fox!" A car pulled up alongside, driven by

a youth in a baseball cap. "Give that Trudi one for me, eh!"

"It's Fox!" Two girls on the other side of the road waved and began to cross, even though the lights had just changed and traffic was pouring towards them. A Japanese tourist turned round and pointed a camera. Cars began to sound their horns. The spell was broken. If Fox stayed still, he would be torn apart by the carrion crowds. He gestured wildly and, as the girls weaved through the traffic and were almost upon him, a taxi pulled up. Fox got in and gave his address. The girls banged on the window but they were too late. He was away.

"You're that Fox, aren't you?" the driver said. Once Fox had stopped hyperventilating, he admitted that he was.

"I had that Trudi Garth in the back of my cab once," the driver went on. "Mean cow. I hope you give a better tip than her."

Fox realized that he'd just given Hunter all his money. He had nothing to pay for the cab with.

"Yeah," he said, "if you could pull up by a cash machine. You know, somewhere quiet."

"No problemmo."

The driver started asking questions which Fox answered monosyllabically. His mind was on Hunter: two grand a week made over a hundred thousand a year. Suppose it took a year to find Sapphire? So what. Fox could afford it. Sapphire was worth it. But suppose she didn't want to be found? Then he'd say hello and leave her alone. He wouldn't tell anyone.

They were at the house. "I'm sorry," Fox said, fumbling in his pocket for his last bit of change. "I don't have enough on me. I asked you to stop at a cash machine."

"Forget it," the cabbie said. "Here." He thrust a book of receipts at Fox. "Sign me a few autographs."

"Sure."

The guy was astute, Fox realized, as he did the tenth one. Genuine Face To Face autographs were rare. The group normally had too much security around them for fans to get near. Each of these signatures would sell for several times the unpaid fare.

"Thanks again," he said, getting out.

"Take my advice," the driver said. "Watch out for that Trudi Garth. She'll have you for supper and spit out what she can't digest. I know her type."

"G'night." Fox went into the house, angry that he'd let the cabbie talk to him like that. He knew that Trudi provoked extreme reactions. She didn't care what most people thought of her. Except she wanted Fox to like her, and he did. But did he trust her? That was a hard one.

29

Face To Face relaunched themselves with a fan-club only concert at the Savoy Theatre. Fox was nervous before the event. They all were. But it was like they'd never been away. Trudi fitted in. She was as good on the old songs as she was on the new ones. *Too Little, Too Late* had been released to the radio stations the day before. The fans already knew it. The song got the best reception of the evening.

Afterwards, there were no screwdrivers in dressing-room doors, no strange events of any kind. The band stayed behind for an hour and a half, signing autographs. When they were through, Trudi hugged Fox.

"That was terrific! You know, it felt really right. Like I belonged with you guys. I can't wait for the tour."

"Me, neither."

Chris and Kerri seemed cheerful, too. They felt like a band again. The group had a few days' holiday, and then the build-up to their second album began in earnest. First, the single, which should be their fourth number one, then the album, then the UK tour, then the USA until, finally, the rest of the world. They would be on tour until the end of the year.

"Going anywhere special?" Fox asked Trudi, kind of hoping that she would ask him along.

The singer smiled. "I dunno. If I have any luck, it'll be somewhere with lots of slim, suntanned, handsome young men."

"I could do with working on a tan myself," Fox quipped, but Trudi didn't take the hint.

"A couple of announcements," Hud said, before Fox could ask Trudi anything else. "We need the track listing of the album finalised before you guys get back from holiday, so if anyone has any input, fax or e-mail me a list before next weekend, all right?"

They all murmured agreement. The album tracks almost chose themselves, Fox thought. They had a dozen really strong ones. He was happy for Hud to choose the running order. The manager had a more detached ear.

"The other thing," Hud went on. "I don't want to send you off on holiday on a bum note, but you're bound to hear. I've just been told the release date of The Ghosts' new single."

"They haven't?" Trudi said, her face turning angry and sour.

"They have. It's coming out on the same day as ours. *Top of the Pops* want to stage a kind of battle of the bands. As far as I'm concerned, we're going to win. But we could put back the release date by a week, if you want. The question is, are you up for it?"

"You bet we are," Fox said. "Whatever The Ghosts've got, it can't beat *Too Little Too Late*."

"We can't be certain," Hud said. "It's not all down to the song. It's as much down to the marketing."

"I've never backed away from a fight in my life," Trudi said. "I'm not going to start now."

Chris and Kerri said nothing. These days, they either spoke with one voice, or they didn't speak at all.

Fox didn't go abroad on holiday. He didn't want a suntan, and he needed to be available if Hunter rang with news about Sapphire. He ended up spending the ten days by himself. He invited a couple of old friends over, but one was working, while the other couldn't take the time off from university. At least, that was what they said. Maybe they had other reasons. He hadn't seen either of them for nearly a year. Fox wanted to form new friendships, but it was easier said than done. Most musicians his age were struggling, and didn't respect what Fox did. Older musicians respected success, but why would they want to hang out with someone half their age?

Fox knew hangers-on who he could invite to spend time with him: record company people, journalists, the in-crowd who he came across in clubs. But he didn't want that kind of shallow company. He'd never been so lonely, he realized. He missed the rest of the band. In particular, he missed Sapphire.

So he sat around for a week, watching the media build up the story of the battle between the bands.

Who's got the biggest? The Trudi factor puts the niggle into the biggest battle of the bands ever!

"Ghosts' single is our best yet," says Tina Toldeo. "We're going to show Trudi what we're made of."

"We never really needed Trudi," Tina said on TV. "In fact, she made our sound too soft."

Fox began to worry. This wasn't about Face To Face and his new song, it was about Trudi versus her old friends turned enemies. As before, he'd shared the publishing of *Too Little, Too Late* with the rest of the band. Now he saw in the press that, as far as the media were concerned, it was Trudi's song. He was forgotten. That made Fox angry.

But not as angry as Chris and Kerri were when Fox finally returned to the house. They'd returned from their holiday early.

"Have you seen this?" Chris asked, thrusting some artwork at Fox. *This* was the cover design for the second Face To Face album. It was bright and cheerful, much like the first album cover.

"It looks all right to me," Fox said.

"Not the cover itself," Kerri told him. "The track listing."

Fox looked. Immediately, he saw what they meant. *Too Little, Too Late* kicked the album off, and there was another of his songs as track nine. He'd been hoping for three. The two songs he'd written with Trudi were there, credited to Fox/Garth. Chris and Kerri had one song each. The remaining five songs on the album were written by, and featured lead vocals by, Trudi Garth.

"This is outrageous!" Fox said.

"You haven't done too badly," Chris commented. "Two songs and two co-credits."

"The co-credits were meant to be B-sides," Fox said. "And I wanted us all to keep sharing the song-writing royalties."

"But look at how the credits read," Kerri said. "Two songs by Garth and Fox, four songs supposedly by all of Face To Face and *five* songs by Trudi Garth. What's anyone going to think?"

"That we're Trudi's band."

"Precisely."

"We've got to get this changed," Chris said.

"I couldn't agree more."

"We've been calling Hud since we got back to the country," Kerri told Fox. "But his machine's on all the time."

"Then we should go straight to the record company."

Fox got on the phone to CPM. It should be a straightforward matter, rearranging the tracks on an album. The three of them quickly agreed to a straightforward split: three songs each. And if Trudi insisted on keeping the publishing on her songs, then they would do the same. Why should she get a share of their stuff if she wasn't willing to share hers?

But the record company wouldn't take their calls. CPM was a small outfit. They were distributed by EMI, but nobody at EMI would change the track listing on the album without the go-ahead from CPM. And nobody at CPM would act without hearing from Hud. Hud *was* CPM. Eventually, the company agreed that they would make the changes if they were agreed by all four members of the band. Trudi was still on holiday.

She returned on a Sunday evening, three days before the TOTP showdown with The Ghosts. At the first rehearsal, Kerri launched into an attack about the track listing on the album.

"It's got nothing to do with me," Trudi protested. "Hud made the decision. If he thinks my songs are the strongest, that's up to him. I'm too close to my material. I can't tell what works and what doesn't."

Fox played conciliator. "Here's what we propose," he said.

Trudi took the new track listing and read it. "Fine by me," she said. "And I'm glad to see that everybody's taking credit for their songs. I'd've been embarrassed if I was the only one keeping my own publishing. Now, can we rehearse?"

Crisis over, they played until interrupted by Fox's mobile. He answered it.

"This is Hunter."

"Hold on, would you?" Fox turned to the others. "I need to take this in my room."

As he left, Fox heard Trudi saying, "It looks like our lead guitarist got himself a girlfriend while we were away."

"What've you got?" Fox asked, when he was alone. He could hear pub sounds in the background before Hunter spoke.

"Less than I hoped. I tracked down one Melanie Duckenfield. She's the right age, but she's not your girl. I'm almost certain that the birth certificate and passport Sapphire showed Hud were phoney. Any chance of a look at the originals?"

"I don't think Hud's got them. He might have taken a copy of her birth certificate."

"See if you can get hold of it. But bear this in mind. Sapphire never really existed. Melanie Duckenfield didn't exist either. You've got me looking for someone who was never really there!"

30

"It's too late to change the track order or the publishing credits," Hud told them on Monday morning. "The CDs are being pressed. Contracts have been signed. I asked for your input while you were on holiday. None of you got back to me. I chose what looked like the strongest running order. You've all got something on there."

"But Trudi wrote half the album!" Chris protested.

"So what? It's the songs that count, not your egos. They were the best songs."

"I don't agree," Fox said. "I think you're trying to change our direction, make us into the Trudi Garth band."

"I want Sapphire back," Kerri said.

"Don't we all?" Hud muttered wryly. "But nobody knows what happened to her. I've paid detective agencies thousands to track her down. No joy. You're about to have a huge hit. You want more of your songs putting out? I'll make up for it on the third album. All right?"

He left the rehearsal before they could reply.

"There won't be a third album at this rate," Kerri said.

"I'm really sorry about this," Trudi said. "Want me to go and talk to him?"

"What's the point?" Fox asked. "You heard the man. The CDs are already being pressed."

"They could melt it down, or whatever…"

"Let's just rehearse," Chris said. "I don't want to talk about this any more."

His confidence had been hurt, Fox saw. He and Kerri were being reduced to sidemen. Fox didn't like being pushed into number two position himself. But then Trudi smiled at him and launched into one of the numbers they'd written together. Fox decided to put aside the petty squabbles. He'd lost less than the others. And he was playing music with one of his all-time heroes.

The single was in the shops. Advance orders for *Too Little, Too Late* had been huge: nearly two hundred thousand. In an ordinary week, a sale of half that number would guarantee a number one. But this wasn't an ordinary week. The new Ghosts single was coming out. *Bring It Down* sounded like a classic rock song from the sixties or seventies.

The Ghosts had a smaller fan base than Face To Face, but Fox reckoned that neutral listeners were more likely to buy *Bring It Down*. This was especially true because the Ghosts single was half price during its first week of release, while Face To Face were charging the full amount. "Otherwise we'd be giving copies away," Hud insisted, when Trudi argued for a price cut. "Don't worry. Discounting shows that they're desperate."

Top of the Pops was recorded on Wednesday afternoon and went out on Friday evening. While committed fans would have bought the single on the day it came out, most impulse buys took place on Saturday. So there was everything to play for.

A limo took Face To Face, together with Hud, Jim and a bodyguard to the studio. Outside, hundreds of fans were waiting: those for The Ghosts on one side of a police line, the Face To Face fans on the other. They were younger, Fox noticed, and nearly all of them girls. They screamed as the band got out of the limo. But not all of the screams were favourable ones.

"Bring back Sapphire!" several yelled.

"We want Trudi dead!" chanted others, and the older fans on the Ghosts' side joined in. Cans and bottles were thrown at her. A Pepsi can hit Fox, bouncing harmlessly off his shoulder. One police officer was less lucky: a missile caught her in the face. Trudi was unscathed.

Then the band were inside. The Ghosts and Face

To Face were to perform one after the other, directly before the chart run-down.

"We thought we'd start the show with Tina and Trudi tossing a coin to decide who goes first," the producer suggested.

Hud looked at Trudi, who was shaking her head. "Thing is," he told the producer, "Trudi and Tina haven't spoken for over a year."

"They don't have to speak now. One of them flips a coin, the other calls *heads* or *tails*. It makes good TV."

"Give us five minutes to talk about it."

Fox watched Hud whispering to Trudi. Why did she hate her old partner so much? He wondered if he would feel the same way about Trudi once he'd been working with her for a while. Fox would be furious if this old rivalry stopped the best song he'd written from getting to number one.

There was a commotion and Fox looked. The Ghosts were arriving. All of them, Fox saw, had been covered with eggs and flour. Tina Toldeo looked furious. A few minutes later, the producer returned.

"Tina won't have anything to do with the coin tossing, so forget it. I'll sort it out with the managers."

Hud followed him to the dressing room. He came back five minutes later, smiling. "We're going second."

Fox wasn't sure if that was a good or a bad thing.

Wouldn't some people turn off after The Ghosts, not giving his song a chance?

"Did Tina have a message for me?" Trudi asked, smiling triumphantly.

"Since you ask," Hud said, "she did. The message was: *Drop dead*!"

"And now," the DJ said, "for the moment you've all been waiting for: *the battle of the bands*! First off, it's their tenth single, but will it be their fifth number one? Please welcome, with *Bring It Down*, The Ghosts!"

Despite the flour attack, Tina and her band looked great. The producer got them to do the song twice. Both versions sounded strong to Fox. If he were watching the show, theirs would be the single he went out and bought, not some sappy ballad about a stupid guy who was too proud to admit that he'd fallen in love.

Would Sapphire be watching on Friday? She *had* to be. She *had* to realize that *Too Little, Too Late* was about her. All that Fox wanted was to get through to Sapphire. He wanted her to know that he still cared.

The band got on to the stage. Fox watched as Kerri took off her engagement ring, in case she damaged it while drumming. Trudi picked up her bass, then, looking at Fox, licked her lips suggestively.

"We're gonna play this like we're in love, right?"

No! Fox thought. That wasn't what he meant at all. In the video, they'd all been filmed separately.

"Face to face, right?" Trudi said. "Heads touching?"

"I don't think so," Fox told her. "I want the audience to think we're singing to *them* not to each other."

"You don't mean the audience," Trudi told him, as the producer asked if they were ready. "You mean Sapphire, don't you?" When Fox didn't reply, she whispered in his ear, "Forget Sapphire, Fox. She's dead."

How could she know that? What did she mean?

"And now," the DJ announced, "in the other corner, featuring former Ghosts member Trudi Garth, are a group waiting to see if they can be the first band *ever* to have their first four singles go straight into the chart at number one. Here, with *Too Little, Too Late* are Face To Face!"

Afterwards, Fox didn't know how he got the words out. The song was a duet, with him and Trudi pouring out their heartache. Were they singing about each other, or about two different love affairs which hadn't worked out – like Fox and Sapphire, or Trudi and The Ghosts? Only the listener could decide.

Fox sang the first two lines of each verse, Trudi the second two.

Time to stop telling lies
I know it's over now
It's time to dry my eyes
Thought we'd make it somehow

If I told you that I loved you
Would the words compensate
Would you blow out my candle
Tell me to put it down to fate

So I've put what went wrong in a song
Wanna be more than your mate
My timing's gone, I can't go on
I gave too little, too late

Too little, too late

They repeated the last line together.

"Fantastic!" the producer said. "We won't be asking you to do it again. That was brilliant!"

They left the studio without exchanging as much as a glance with Tina Toldeo and The Ghosts.

"How do you know?" Fox asked Trudi in the limousine. "How do you know that Sapphire's dead?"

Trudi, for once in her life, looked embarrassed.

"I don't know anything," she said. "I said what I said to get a reaction, to make you give the song everything. It worked, didn't it?"

* * *

On Friday night, Fox stayed in. He was hoping that, after seeing the show, Sapphire would call. If she was alive, she couldn't stay hidden for ever. The press would pick up the story of her disappearance, track her down.

If she wasn't alive … Fox didn't want to think about it.

Sapphire didn't call.

On Sunday, *Too Little, Too Late* entered the chart at number two. *Bring It Down* had outsold it by 13,000 copies. Somehow, Trudi managed to be a good loser. Live on the radio, she talked about the new direction and focus she'd given to Face To Face. *Too Little, Too Late* was only the first example of that, she said.

"Just wait till you hear the songs I've written for the album," she said. "They'll blow you away."

Fox felt like killing her.

31

Despite Trudi's confidence, Face To Face's second album wasn't as well received as the first. Critics attacked it, the *NME* calling Trudi Garth's songs "cynical attempts to write trashy teen-fodder". A large proportion of their fans seemed to be waiting for Sapphire to return.

Hud had changed the marketing strategy for the group. Chris and Kerri were the "nice" ones. Fox and Trudi were the "nasty" couple. On tour, Fox got to wear leather like Trudi, and act the guitar god during his solos. Fox had long since stopped trusting Trudi. Every night, he tried to upstage her. It made for a good show.

Fans were divided over whether they liked the new image. Many hated Trudi. But there was no violence on the tour. The group were still huge. Massive success insulated them from crazy fans and over-zealous reporters alike. They travelled every-where by private plane, performed in sports arenas and stadiums, then were whisked away to stay in penthouse suites.

It was a lonely, lunatic existence. Fox was still distanced from Chris and Kerri. Off-stage, Trudi was aloof. She looked rock 'n' roll, but didn't act it: going to bed early, spending her recreation time shopping in stores which opened specially for her. Fox decided that everything about Trudi was an act. She was an old-fashioned ballad singer pretending to be a rebellious rock 'n' roller. Chris and Kerri were more rebellious than she was.

Not only that, but – as far as Fox was concerned – Trudi's songs weren't all that good. They always got the smallest cheers of the night, though Trudi seemed not to notice. One of her songs was slated as their fifth single. Fox didn't rate it.

Stories had started to appear about Sapphire's disappearance. It was over six months now and no-body knew where she was. When asked about her, the band always told reporters: *She's having a rest. She'll come back when she's ready*. But none of them believed it.

Maybe they should tell the truth, Fox thought. Hunter hadn't come up with anything new. He phoned regularly, always asking Fox if he wanted him to continue. Fox was probably throwing his money away, but he couldn't break faith now. Not unless there was another way.

If the press got the story that Sapphire had vanished without trace, maybe they'd find out what had happened to her. Trouble was, publicity could have the opposite effect, ensuring that Sapphire never surfaced again. Was it worth the risk? Fox didn't know who he could discuss it with. Certainly not Hud or Trudi.

"Kerri thinks that Sapphire's dead," Chris told Fox on the plane, when everyone around them was sleeping.

"Why?" Fox asked. "There's no evidence that—"

"Except what happened to Art, then to Alan Mackay."

"Art had a hole in his heart. Alan Mackay was probably murdered by drug dealers. Sapphire told Hud that she was leaving the band."

"Or so he said," Chris responded.

Fox gave Chris an incredulous look. "You're saying that Hud might have killed Sapphire? That's ridiculous. He's our manager. If you don't trust him, then…"

Chris hushed him. Hud was asleep three rows ahead of them. "I'm not saying that Sapphire's dead. That's what Kerri reckons, but I think she's being paranoid."

So did Fox. He couldn't bear the thought of never seeing Sapphire again.

"Look," Chris said, "Face To Face is your first big break, right?"

"Right," Fox agreed. "So what?"

"So I've been around a bit longer, waiting for my chance. You get to find out things. The record business has as many crooks as other businesses. More, because there's so much money involved. Did you get a lawyer to look at the contract you signed with Face To Face?"

"No," Fox confessed.

"It stinks. I had it looked at and found that there were all sorts of tricks, like, if I get ill and have to leave the band, I get nothing. When you get right down to it, we're Hud's employees. I saw a solicitor, tried to make some changes. No joy. Hud told me to take it or leave it.

"I needed the gig. So I signed. The point I'm making is – if you want to succeed, you can't have too many scruples or unrealistic expectations."

Fox still wasn't sure exactly what Chris was getting at.

"So what do you think's happened to Sapphire?" he asked.

"I don't know," Chris said. "And I don't want to know."

Later, Fox tried talking to Jim, the security chief. "Where do you think she is?" he asked, after they'd reminisced about Sapphire for a few minutes.

"Probably in the Bahamas, sunning herself. She cleaned out her account, did you hear that?"

"No," Fox said. "Couldn't you trace the money?"

"Why?" Jim asked. "Sapphire hasn't done anything illegal, far as I know. The inland revenue might be after her, but apart from that…"

"Why do you think she left?" Fox asked.

"You'd have to ask her," Jim said, with an edgy grin.

"Do you think Hud knows?"

"No idea," Jim grunted.

"The phone call that Hud says Sapphire made, when she said she was quitting because of the pressure. Were you there when he got that?"

"No," Jim said, "I wasn't. Look, I'm not comfortable with all these questions. Go ask Hud, why don't you?"

But Fox wasn't ready to confront Hud. He suspected that the manager had forced Sapphire out. Maybe he had even had her killed. Maybe he had had Art killed, too, and Alan Mackay. As Chris said, there was a lot of money involved, and all that Hud seemed to care about was money. But Sapphire was the most popular member of the band before she left. She was a better songwriter and, potentially, a better musician than Trudi. Why would Hud want to get rid of her? Fox was probably only being paranoid.

"Ladies and gentlemen," the manager said, at their band meeting the next day, "here it is: your next single!"

He passed out advance copies. "It'll be in the shops in a week."

"Hold on," Kerri said. "I was saving this song for the next album."

Fox took a look at the track list. The A-side was an album track, *Free Me*, written by Trudi. The other songs were ones which had been missed off the second album in favour of Trudi Garth songs: one from each of them.

"Think of it as an EP," Hud said. "One song from each of you. I thought you'd be pleased."

"I see what you're up to," Chris said. "We need a number one. All of our fans have already bought the album with *Free Me* on it, so you need three good new songs to make sure they'll buy the song again."

"Precisely," Hud said. "We might get a number one without these new songs. In the summer, you don't need to sell as many singles to get to the top. But I don't want to take any chances."

"Hey!" Kerri said. "I've got an even better idea."

"What?"

"Why don't we make one of the other songs the A-side? A new song's more likely to go to number one. And the other numbers are all better than Trudi's anyhow."

"Pardon?" Trudi said. She and Fox had been sitting the discussion out until now. "You don't think *Free Me*'s a number one?"

The discussion degenerated into a row. As they ran out of steam, Hud pulled his usual trick of telling the group that it was too late to change the plans anyway. They were stuck with it.

"Look, Trudi," Fox said when he was gone. "I think we need to discuss this. The choice of single should be a band decision, not Hud's."

"Read your contract," Trudi said. "The manager has a final say on all matters to do with musical content. Look, I'm sorry, I've got to go. A date."

"Brian Costigan?" Chris asked.

Trudi gave him one of her *wouldn't you like to know* looks, then left. According to the tabloids, Trudi was dating Costigan, the lead guitarist of a well-known hard-rock band. But Fox had only seen the couple together once, and the guy hadn't shown up at all during the US tour. He knew better than to believe what he read in the papers.

Over the past year and a bit, Fox had been linked with Kerri, Sapphire, Trudi, a Breakfast TV presenter, an ex-Spice Girl, a German tennis player and two page three girls, not to mention a Member of Parliament twice his age, who'd persuaded him to sign a letter protesting about North Sea pollution. Even after their engagement, Chris and Kerri had both been linked with other people. There was no point in getting upset over the stories. Gossip, it seemed, made the world go round.

"What about *Top of the Pops*?" Chris asked.

"I'm not doing it," Kerri said. "Why should we be seen as Trudi's backing group? We can send the video."

"Have you seen the video?" Chris asked. "It's all Trudi anyhow."

"You're being childish," Fox said. "Why risk messing our career up?"

"I don't care any more," Kerri said. "Being top isn't everything. You know, after we perform at Wembley on Sunday, I think I might quit."

"If you go, I go too," Chris said.

"Read your contract," Fox told them. "Quit the group and you lose all your future royalties. Hud gets the money that's rightfully yours."

"Maybe he deserves it," Kerri said. "We're an image, not a real group. Hud created us. He can replace us. You stay, Fox. Play with Trudi on *Top of the Pops*. I'm not sure how much more I can stand. If we hadn't already agreed to do the Wembley thing, I'd go now."

The Wembley gig was a massive charity event, featuring all of the biggest British acts of the moment. Fox couldn't remember what the cause was – they'd agreed to it six months ago. He did remember that the show had sold out in half an hour and the BBC were showing it live on the very day that *Free Me* would enter the chart. Face To Face were headlining over The Ghosts and a dozen other major acts.

"No," Fox said. "If you won't do *Top of the Pops*, then neither will I. But I think you're cutting off your nose to spite your face."

"We've had enough," Chris said. "It isn't fun any more."

"It was never about fun," Fox said. "You told me that. It's about making lots of money."

"You're right," Kerri agreed. "But we've all made lots of money. How much more do you need?"

Fox couldn't answer that.

"We've hired a lawyer," Chris told Fox. "He's examining our contracts. I want to set up a meeting with Hud on Monday, once the Wembley gig's out of the way."

"A meeting to do what?" Fox asked. "Break up the band?"

But Chris and Kerri didn't answer.

32

Stephanie got off the bus and began the short walk home. Nigel Brown accompanied her for a couple of minutes, trying to work up to asking her out, as usual. Stephanie always managed to head him off before he actually asked, therefore saving him the humiliation of an outright rejection and her the embarrassment of delivering it.

They talked about their English A-level lesson and how useless Thursday night TV was. Then Nigel mentioned the weekend. Stephanie started moaning about some imaginary relatives she had to visit, keeping the story going until it was time for Nigel to turn off.

At least Nigel was interested. Since changing her name and cutting her hair, Stephanie hadn't exactly been overwhelmed by offers from boys. The rumours about her nervous breakdown hadn't helped, but she'd needed some explanation as to why she'd been gone from school for so long that she'd had to drop back a year.

Most girls saw Steph's short, severe haircut and assumed that she was trying to put off boys. Most boys decided that she'd gone lesbian. Many thought that she'd had a baby, or an abortion. Steph neither confirmed nor denied any of the rumours. As long as nobody guessed the truth, she didn't mind what they thought.

Steph was usually the first to get home. Dad worked late, and Mum, a teacher, often had meetings after school. But today Mum was already in, and she wasn't alone. The man in the kitchen was portly and wore a long black leather coat. Beneath his heavy-rimmed black glasses, he had pig-like, Billy Bunter eyes.

"Mr Hunter's come to ask a few questions about Melanie," Mum said.

"Why? What's going on? Is Melanie in trouble at university?"

"Please sit down, Stephanie," the man said. "This won't take long."

Mum looked anxious. She'd never been happy about the whole thing, but was so glad to have Steph back that she hadn't argued about what she'd done.

"I met your sister a few months ago," the fat man said, "but she wasn't the person I was looking for."

"Are you a journalist?" Steph asked, suspiciously.

"No, I'm a private investigator. And, I assure you, I'm very discreet."

"Who's employing you?" Steph asked.

"I'm not at liberty to say. Not yet, anyway."

"What do you want?"

"Where were you last year, Stephanie?" the fat man asked.

"None of your business," Steph said.

"That, I'm afraid, is where you're wrong. You see, I've been looking for you for several months now, and my client has spent a small fortune on my services."

"How do you know that I'm who you're looking for?"

The man who called himself "Hunter" gave a comic shrug. "You could come out and admit it. That would be the easiest way. Or I could take your fingerprints, compare them with the ones that you gave to the police when they arrested you for cocaine possession."

"I don't know who you're confusing me with," Steph said. "But you're talking crazy. I ran away from home when I was sixteen and lived rough in London for a while. Then I came to my senses, returned home and started doing my A-levels." That was the story she'd agreed with her family in the event of anyone asking questions like this.

"A nice tale," the fat man said, "and more or less true, except for the details you left out. Like borrowing your sister's passport to prove that you were over eighteen and therefore entitled to sign a recording contract. Her birth certificate, too, I believe. You travelled to America, pretending to be her, even though you're two and a half years younger and don't look remotely alike. That took some nerve, I must say, Stephanie."

Steph took a deep breath then looked to her mother for help. Mum shook her head. "Or may I call you *Sapphire*?" the fat man asked.

"That was very petty," Hud complained on Thursday evening, "not showing up for *Top of the Pops*."

"You should have consulted us over the single," Fox said. "It was the last straw. Sorry."

"If we don't go straight in at number one, it'll be your fault."

Fox ignored this. He'd agreed to broach a difficult subject. "Listen, Hud. The day after the Wembley gig, we want a meeting: the four of us, you, your lawyer, Trudi's lawyer, our lawyer."

"*What?*" The manager sounded outraged. "Call in lawyers and they'll swallow all the money," Hud said. "They always do."

"We'll take that risk," Fox said.

"Are you quitting?" Hud asked, beginning to sound rattled.

"I'll talk to you on Monday," Fox said. "Don't call me before then. In fact, I'm disconnecting my mobile."

He hung up. With the phone disconnected, Hunter wouldn't be able to get in touch with him, but he hadn't heard from him for ages anyway.

*　*　*

If Fox stayed in the house, Hud or Trudi would seek him out. Fox didn't want that. They were supposed to be rehearsing for Sunday's show, but it hardly mattered. Face To Face had played so many shows this year that they were note perfect.

As Fox strummed absent-mindedly on his guitar, a van arrived to collect Chris and Kerri's stuff. From today, they were renting a flat in Chelsea. Fox was the only person left in the house. He ought to get a place of his own. After Monday, he was going to need one.

But what would he do without the band? He had no other life. Some teen stars, he knew, took a break and turned normal. They went to university. But Fox had rubbish GCSEs and had never taken A-levels. That wasn't an option. His only opportunities were in music. Pop music. After being in Face To Face, no one would take him seriously if he tried to do something more credible.

Fox needed somebody to work with. But not Chris and Kerri. And certainly not Trudi. Off-stage, there was no rapport between them. Fox had to strike out on his own.

Unless, that was, Hunter managed to find Sapphire. Reluctantly, Fox had come to a conclusion: either Sapphire was dead, or she didn't want to be found. He would never see her again.

Fox went to pack his stuff. He'd stay in a hotel for the next few days, he decided, then make up his mind where to go next.

On Friday evening, Stephanie sat down to watch *Top of the Pops*. Mr Hunter had explained who'd hired him. He'd also told her that nobody else knew about his enquiries. So she'd been expecting Fox to call, but it hadn't happened yet. Face To Face had a new single out. Maybe Fox was distracted.

Then there was that big Wembley show on Sunday. Sapphire – sorry, Stephanie, she must stop thinking of herself as *Sapphire* – would have been scared witless by the prospect of playing to a hundred thousand people. Maybe Fox was, too.

She missed him, actually. She was sorry that she'd left without saying goodbye. But Fox might have persuaded her to stay. And she couldn't do that. She couldn't have carried on the pretence a minute longer.

Top of the Pops began. As usual, they saved the "*Face To Face Exclusive!*" until nearly the end of the show, so that fans didn't turn over or turn off. When the band's slot arrived, Stephanie was stunned. They weren't there.

Trudi Garth stood in a single spotlight, singing a ghastly song about *being free*. No explanation was given for the absence of the rest of the band. The presenter finished by reminding viewers that Face To Face's final UK performance of the year would be shown live on TV the following Sunday evening.

"But will *Free Me* put them back at number one? Tune in on Sunday to the only chart that counts, and find out!"

What had happened to the band? Stephanie went to the phone and dialled the house number. It rang for ages without an answer. Mr Hunter had given her Fox's mobile number. She tried that. A recorded message told her that the machine was switched off. She should try again later.

Stephanie didn't need a sixth sense to know that something was wrong.

On Saturday evening, Lianne boarded the overnight coach to London. Nobody knew where she was going. Her parents were out for the evening. Lianne's medication made her sleep late, so they were unlikely to check her room much before midday. By then, she would be at the front of the queue, waiting to be let into Wembley Stadium. She'd be wearing a black jumpsuit, for old time's sake. But she wouldn't be carrying a screwdriver.

Lianne had been on a home visit three months ago when she'd sneaked her mum's credit card, spent three hours on the phone and finally secured a ticket for tomorrow's show. Now she was free, cured. Lianne had convinced the doctors that she was a normal teenager.

True, she'd promised that she wouldn't go near Face To Face in future, but they couldn't expect her to miss an event like this, could they? From what Lianne had seen on last night's *Top of the Pops*, tomorrow might be the group's last performance.

She just had to be there.

33

"Wembley Stadium," Fox told the taxi driver. Face To Face were due on stage at nine-thirty, just as the sun went down. Fox had been watching the concert on TV in his hotel room: half enjoying it, half horrified. He was too young to remember *Live Aid* but imagined it must have been like this: all the country's top bands, trying to be better than the rest. The prospect of going on stage after them, in front of all those people, was absolutely terrifying.

He'd spoken to Chris and Kerri on the phone. They'd been having meetings with lawyers all weekend.

"We'd have invited you along," Chris said, "but we didn't know where to find you. Your mobile's—"

"It's all right," Fox said. "I'll leave that side up to you."

He had no desire to meet money-grubbing lawyers. Nor did he want to spend day after day in court, fighting for his rights in a group he was growing to hate. Tonight, one way or another, would be their final performance.

"But you'll come to the meeting Monday?" Chris asked.

"I'll be there," Fox had said.

Now the taxi driver recognized him. "You in that Face To Face?"

"Yeah."

"Thought it was you. That Trudi Garth, she's all right, but she's no Sapphire, know what I mean?"

"I know exactly what you mean," Fox said. He wasn't in the mood for small talk, and he'd remembered something. "Would you mind putting Radio One on, please?"

The chart run-down had reached number four.

"You got a new single out, then?"

"Yes," Fox said.

"My daughter likes you. She says you always go in at number one."

"Not this time," Fox said, wondering whether it was true. *Free Me* wasn't at number four. It wasn't at number three, either.

"Could you go to the artists' entrance?" Fox asked.

"Yeah. So, number one or number two, eh?"

"I expect our single's already been on. We probably missed it." Fox didn't *want* to be number one, he realized, especially not with a Trudi Garth song. He hoped that last week's number one, a dance record, had held on to the top spot.

"Here we are."

There were a group of girls waiting outside. "Keep the change," Fox said, handing over a twenty.

"Aren't you going to wait to see if…"

But Fox was already out of the car. Teenage girls clustered around him, trying to get his autograph. Fox was early. He'd sign them all.

"Can you get us in?" one of the girls asked.

"Sorry, it's for charity, so there's no guest list."

"How about me?" asked a familiar voice. "Any chance of getting me in?" Fox looked up and, for a moment, didn't recognize her. She had short hair, sunglasses, no make-up. She wore jeans and a T-shirt. She could be one of a million seventeen-year-old girls. Except she wasn't.

"Sapphire!" he shouted, and hugged her.

"Not so loud. I'm trying to be incognito these days."

"Where've you…?"

"I'll tell you later. Can we go inside?"

Fox told the gate security that Sapphire was his girlfriend.

"Call me Stephanie from now on," she told Fox. "Steph, for short. It's my name. Think the others'll recognize me?"

"Let's see." Fox put an arm around Stephanie and walked into the backstage area. It looked like a *Who's Who* of modern rock and pop music.

"This is Steph," he said, introducing her to several musicians who'd met Sapphire before. None of them knew who she was. Chris, Kerri and Trudi were nowhere in sight.

"Why did you find me now?" Fox asked, when they were alone.

"You sent that guy to look for me. He's been trying to contact you for days. So have I."

Fox explained why he'd made himself incommunicado. "But what I want to know," he finished, "is why you quit the band."

"I didn't quit," Stephanie said. "I was sacked."

On stage, The Who had reformed, and were playing *Won't Get Fooled Again*. Fox and Stephanie found a seat away from the monitors where they could hear each other speak without having to shout.

"Hud found out the truth," Steph told him. "I was only sixteen when I joined the group. You had to be over eighteen. I had two parents and an elder sister. Hud wanted orphans. So I lied: told him I'd been living rough for a long time – borrowed my big sister's birth certificate when he needed proof of age for the contracts.

"The trouble came once we started going abroad. I borrowed Melanie's passport – nobody examines it properly when you're famous, which is a good thing because she doesn't look much like me. But I was getting worried about breaking the law. And I was fed up of lying. You'd started wanting to get close and I couldn't take it, not while I was pretending like that. That's why I knocked you back."

"So what happened?" Fox asked.

"I went home for Christmas, talked it over with my parents and Melanie. We figured it was time for me to come clean. But when I rang Hud and told him, he exploded. Said I'd betrayed him, that I was too young to tour and he'd cut me off without a penny of royalties.

"When Dad tried to talk to him, Hud said he'd sue him out of house and home unless I vanished completely. If I did that, I could keep the royalties that were coming to me. By then, I'd had enough. I'd seen what being a rock star was like – how empty the whole thing was. I'd got more than enough money to see me through university and set me up in whatever I decide to do afterwards. I haven't given up the idea of music completely, but…"

She stopped speaking and made her face become a mask of blandness. Fox looked round.

"Who's the lucky girl?" Trudi Garth asked, bouncing over as though everything was right in the world.

"This is Steph. Steph, this is Trudi." Steph shook hands with Trudi as though they hadn't met before.

"Did you hear the news? *Free Me* went straight in at number one! We're back on top!"

34

There was no glimmer of recognition in Trudi's eyes. *She doesn't know me without all my make-up and hair*, Steph thought. Since returning home, only two people had mentioned that she resembled Sapphire, and then only in a jokey way. One boy had told her that, if she grew her hair long like Sapphire's, he might ask her out. She'd replied that, if he grew his hair really long, she might use it to strangle him with.

Up close, Trudi Garth looked old, tense. Since leaving the band, Stephanie had been doing some digging about the star's history. Trudi was eight years older than she claimed to be. The Ghosts weren't her first band. That was The Tempest Twins, an electro–pop duo. Back then, Trudi used her real name: Sandra Garth. The Tempest Twins had released three singles and an album, *The Matt-Black Dream Home*, with little success.

After The Tempest Twins, Trudi/Sandra learnt guitar and played in a heavy metal band for a while. At one of their gigs, she met Tina Toldeo, a university student several years younger than her. They formed The Ghosts and slowly ground their way to success. Sandra changed her name, took a few years off her age and claimed to have met Tina while a student at university. That kind of fiction was common in rock music, where few journalists bothered to check their facts beyond looking at a record company press release.

What was next for Trudi, Steph wondered? Thanks to Face To Face, she was a superstar at last. She could do anything. Right now, the singer was showing Fox a set list.

"We'll have to see if the others agree," Fox was saying. "I would have thought that Chris and Kerri will want another song each."

"We've only got three-quarters of an hour," Trudi pointed out.

"And what's this?" Fox said, incredulously. "*Dying For You?* We never play that. It was Art's song."

"I thought it was kind of appropriate for the closer," Trudi said, in a wheedling voice. "Seeing as the concert's about people dying in famines and all that."

"But *Dying For You*'s a love song."

"It's also the group's most popular song," Trudi argued.

That wasn't true, Steph thought. *Too Little, Too Late* was her favourite. It made her want to cry every time she heard it. *The Spirit Lives* had been the group's biggest hit. *Dying For You* only brought back memories of Art's death.

"We're mad, not playing it," Trudi added.

"It would be disrespectful to Art," Fox said. "And, anyway, we haven't rehearsed the song. It's over a year since we last played *Dying For You*. You've never played it."

"Wrong," Trudi said. "I've been rehearsing an acoustic version. I thought that I could take lead vocal and you three could do back-up."

Fox was more of a diplomat than Sapphire had been. He accepted that he was making compromises to be a success, and avoided offending anyone. But now he blew his top.

"Listen, tonight might be our last performance. This group's gone to hell since you joined."

"We're the most successful—"

"Shut up!" Fox told her. "I'd give back every number one to have Art alive and Sapphire still here. We all would."

"Oh, forget Art," Trudi snarled. "The kid always knew that he didn't have long to live. Hud gave him a few months in the limelight and he was grateful."

Fox slapped her across the face and Trudi reeled. "How dare—?"

"You're telling me that Hud planned his death? Where is he? I'll…" But the manager was nowhere to be seen. One of the Wembley organizers ran over, obviously worried by the row in progress.

"You're on in twenty minutes. The dressing room's free now, if you'd like to…"

"Thanks," Trudi said, getting up and hurrying off before Fox could say anything. "I'm on my way."

"Where are Chris and Kerri?" the organizer asked.

"I expect they're with our manager," Fox said, cynically. "Have you seen him?"

"I think Hud's up in the box, talking to the Prince of Wales. But the other two aren't there. Would you like me to—?"

"No need," Fox interrupted. "Here they are. We'll be ready on time."

Both Chris and Kerri looked less than happy to be there.

"We wouldn't have turned up if this wasn't for charity," Kerri said. "Is she…?"

"In the dressing room," Fox said. "We had a row. She wanted to sing *Dying For You* virtually solo."

"You're kidding," Chris said. "I … Kerri, what's wrong?"

The drummer was staring. "Sapphire," she said. "Is that you?"

"It's me all right," Stephanie told her.

"I'm so glad you're back," Kerri said. She hugged her. Then Chris hugged her.

"Will you play with us tonight?" Kerri asked.

"I'd love to," Steph said, "but I was thrown out of the band. I don't belong."

"Thrown out?" Chris said. "I thought you walked out."

Sapphire explained.

"This is it then," Chris said, when she was through. "The end of the group. Tonight, we call it quits. I don't care what the lawyers say tomorrow. I don't care how much money they hold back. I'm not working with Hud and Trudi any more."

"Me neither," Fox said.

"What say we tie Trudi up in the dressing room," Kerri suggested, "take Sapphire on stage with us instead of her?"

"It's tempting," Fox agreed.

But Stephanie wouldn't let them. "I'm not rehearsed," she said. "I don't look the part, either. Go play with Trudi."

The organizer was approaching again, pointing at his watch.

"We need you on the revolving stage five minutes before Oasis finish," he pointed out.

"We're on our way," Chris said, reluctantly getting up.

"Maybe we'll get to play together again," Fox said. "Not as Face To Face, since Hud owns the name, but … who knows?"

"Who knows?" Sapphire agreed.

Chris and Kerri headed to the dressing room. Fox lingered.

"Where will you be afterwards?" he asked.

"I'll watch from the side of the stage," she said. "You'll see me."

"I know this is the wrong time and everything but…"

He hesitated. Steph knew what he was going to say. She put her arms around him and kissed his lips for the first time.

"Tell me later," she said. "Now go and play guitar."

35

"*And now, for our final act of the evening. Please give a wonderful Wembley welcome to Face To Face!*"

The band came on and played their theme song. It was a little ragged, but, beneath the screams and hysteria, no one could tell. In the dressing room earlier, the discussion about the set list had been short and terse. Finally, they'd agreed on four of the five hits (not including *Dying For You*) and two more songs each. No one mentioned that this would be their last performance together, but they all knew it.

Three songs in, Trudi stepped forward for her biggest moment.

"This is a song I wrote about some old associates of mine. Sometimes, you have to take risks if you want to be yourself. This is *Free Me*."

Trudi had never introduced the song that way

before. As she sang the opening lines, Fox figured she was trying to tell the world something.

You tie me down
You hold me back
You mess me round
Knock me off track

You let me down
Always keep score
This time I win
Can't take any more

Free me
Before this gets rough
Free me
We've all had enough

He hoped that Trudi wouldn't try and announce that this was the end of the group. If anyone did that, it should be one of the founder members: him or Kerri. Really though, the decision ought to wait until after tomorrow's meeting.

When she was done, Trudi gave a small bow, then stepped back. The spotlight fell on Kerri, and she sang her song from the new EP. It got as good a reception as Trudi's number.

Trudi would go solo, Fox realized. That was what would happen next. She might fail, or she might be the biggest solo star since Madonna. You could never tell. Could he persuade Stephanie to come back, relaunch the group as it used to be? No. They'd all had enough.

It wasn't always the most talented writer, or the one with the best voice who went the furthest. It was sometimes the one with the most ambition or the best manager or even the band member who was the most ruthless. It might just be the one who was best-looking. Until she left, Fox had always thought that it would be Sapphire.

Fox did his song. Normally, he managed to lose himself in the singing, but, tonight, he found himself looking around. The sun had nearly set. Despite the stage lights, he could just about see the faces of the front row of the audience. A couple of them were fans who he'd seen at many shows. That blonde girl looked particularly familiar...

Remembering something, Fox got a line wrong as he turned around, looking for Jim, or someone from security. He only saw Hud, who had come side-stage and was watching the performance. Sapphire – or Stephanie - was nowhere in sight. The song ended. Chris did his number. Trudi did another of hers. Fox looked at the set list taped to the monitor. There was only one song left. He stepped forward, unsure what he was going to say.

"This is the last number," he mumbled. "Thanks for coming. Thanks everybody for watching. Keep donating money..."

And suddenly, for the first time that evening, it

was quiet. Even before he announced the song, the audience had started holding lighters aloft. They knew what the band were going to play. It might not have made number one, but it was the best thing they'd done. Fox stared out at the thousands and thousands of people. He thought about the millions and millions watching on TV. He had a little more to say.

"Tonight is Face To Face's last performance," he said. "After tonight, we break up."

The noise in response was ominous: a kind of rumbling, disbelieving *no* – sad, not angry, almost as though the audience suddenly realized that this had been inevitable all along.

"I wrote this song for Sapphire," Fox finished. "I know she's watching. This is for you. *Too Little, Too Late*."

The audience exploded. Fox had to play the introduction twice before the noise subsided sufficiently for him to hear himself singing. Somehow, surrounded by a constellation of tiny flames, he got through the song, thanked the audience, and left the stage.

Stephanie watched in tears. Then Fox was running towards her. The audience were going crazy and Fox was holding her, repeating "I love you" again and again.

"I love you, too," she told him.

Kerri and Chris were smiling. Only Trudi Garth

looked less than happy. Fox had upstaged her at the end. She'd hinted that she was leaving the band, but Fox had told the whole world that it was over. As the crowd continued to go crazy, the organizer ran over. "We need an encore."

"We haven't rehearsed anything," Chris said. "Shouldn't there be some kind of big singalong? I thought that was how these things ended."

"Please," the organizer said.

Trudi grabbed his shoulder. "It's all right, we've got something. Just mike-up one acoustic guitar."

"What's going on?" Chris asked, as the organizer ran over to the road crew. Fox broke away from Sapphire and asked the same question. He seemed to remember something. "Listen," he said. "I don't want to scare anybody, but…"

Then he saw Trudi, acoustic guitar in hand, walking out on to the stage, a single spotlight picking her out.

"Hey!" he called out. "We never said…"

Hud gave him a sour look. "You just broke up the group, idiot. From now on, what Trudi does is up to her."

Before Fox could reply, Hud walked away. Jim waited a moment, looking at Stephanie as if he half-recognized her, then he, too, went to the other side of the stage, disappearing into the darkness.

Trudi was making a speech about orphans. The audience was impatient. They wanted a feelgood finish, but Trudi was intent on her showstopper ballad. She began to sing the words of *Dying For You* and the audience calmed down, as though willing her to perform magic.

It's a crazy notion
We could go so high
Unleashed emotion
Don't let it go by

The song didn't suit her voice at all, Stephanie thought. It had been written with Art in mind, and, as Trudi reached the chorus, she couldn't hit the high notes.

I'm dying for you
Can't live if you're not near
Oh yes, I'm dying for you
Kill me if I'm not sincere

As she sang the words, Trudi looked around. She was hoping that the others would appear behind her, sing harmonies to drown out her failings. But the rest of Face To Face stood beside Stephanie, silent, like mesmerized onlookers at a car crash. Trudi began another verse.

Then it happened. The audience began to make a high-pitched noise, which nobody on stage understood at first. The event was easiest to understand on television. Trudi looked up to see a large black shape falling towards her. It was swinging across the length of the stage, hence the reaction from the audience, who saw it coming.

The TV camera was hurtling towards Trudi at tremendous velocity. Even so, Trudi managed to step out of the way. For a split second, the look on her face changed from fear to a kind of relief. The camera missed her head by inches. But Trudi hadn't noticed the heavy electrical wire which was attached to it. She'd moved the right way to avoid the big camera, but, in doing so, had stepped into more danger.

The wire cut cleanly through Trudi's neck, decapitating her in front of three hundred and fifty million TV viewers. The BBC's transmission was shut off moments later, but not before the TV screen had shown Trudi's bloody head bounce several times across the stage, then drop and disappear into the frenzied, hysterical crowd.

36

"I thought I saw the screwdriver girl," Fox told the investigating officer at the police station. He explained who he meant. "It might have had something to do with her."

"Do you mean that teenager over there?" The detective pointed at a nervous-looking kid who was perched on a bench in the police station.

"Yes," Fox said. She looked older than he remembered, but he'd never got a good look at her before. "Why's she here?"

"Not sure. Maybe she's giving herself up."

The police were currently treating Trudi's death as "suspicious". The camera which nearly hit Trudi had not been operating. It was an old-fashioned back-up for the lightweight digital cameras which were being used for the broadcast. Either it fell of its own accord, or somebody had climbed up a narrow metal ladder while Trudi was singing, detached the video camera, then aimed the thing at Trudi as though it were a weapon.

"Have you any idea why someone might have had a motive to do this?"

"Not really," Fox said. Still in shock, he blurted out, "Mind you, she was murdering our song."

Nobody laughed. Fox wasn't a suspect. He, Stephanie, Kerri and Chris had been standing together. They were each other's alibi. Hud and Jim were together at the other side of the stage. Neither had seen anything before the disaster occurred.

Lianne was led into an interview room, a cramped space with two chairs, a table, a tape recorder and toilet-green walls. The woman waiting to ask questions had a file in front of her.

"This is you?" she asked. "Lianne Hobbs? You attacked Trudi Garth with a sharpened screwdriver in a hotel car park last year?"

"Yes," Lianne admitted. "I did."

"Perhaps you could start by telling me why you did that."

Lianne took a deep breath. "A psychiatrist could explain it better than I can. My boyfriend had a crush on Trudi Garth. I became fixated on her, obsessed, you could say. I thought that everything that was wrong with my life was Trudi's fault. So I decided to kill her. It seemed to make sense at the time."

"But you didn't succeed?"

"No, I was sectioned under the mental health act, then released into the community two weeks ago."

"With a condition that you didn't go near Trudi."

"I know," Lianne said. "I shouldn't have been there tonight. I'm sorry. But I did see who did this."

The detective looked at her sceptically. Lianne was probably their main suspect. But she wasn't worried.

"Tell me."

"He climbed up the – what do you call it?"

"Lighting rig."

"That's right – just as Trudi came back on stage on her own. I didn't think anything of it. You know, I just thought that he was doing his job. Then Trudi began this embarrassing speech about orphans or something, and I just had to look away. It was bringing back all these feelings of hatred that I thought I'd been cured of. That's when I saw him do it."

"Do what?"

"I stared at the sky. He was leaning over the camera, loosening it, I guess. I think he was holding a knife. Then he started getting rid of the tape, or whatever held it in place. Trudi was singing the song when I saw him reach out. He held the camera, cut something else, then swung it towards her."

"Did you see what happened next?"

"Yes. You know, I was curious, but I still didn't know he'd done anything wrong. I thought it was part of the show. He let go of the camera, then started back down the rope ladder he'd climbed up. I don't know where he went after that. People started screaming and I looked at the stage just in time to see, to see…"

The detective stopped her and gave her a glass of water.

"Would you recognize him again?"

"Yes," Lianne said. "I've seen him before."

"Where?"

"In Glasgow, after a Face To Face gig. I was with this photographer called Alan Mackay."

"The one who died?"

"Yes. Alan was following Face To Face around. He usually slept in his car, but he was waiting for somebody outside the tour bus, which was where I was hiding. He spotted me and we got talking. Alan was celebrating. He'd got these great photos and he was very proud of how clever he'd been. The photos were going to make his fortune."

"How was he celebrating?" the detective asked. She was trying to disguise her mood, but the prospect of solving another murder obviously excited her.

"Cocaine. Alan offered me some, actually."

"Did you take it?"

"Yes," Lianne admitted, "but I didn't use it. I don't like drugs. I planted the coke on Sapphire the next day, because I wanted to get her into trouble. Then he told me to hide. This guy came along and asked Alan to go for a walk with him."

"The same guy on the lighting rig?"

"Yes. The next thing I heard was that Alan was dead."

"Why didn't you tell the police at the time?"

"And explain what I was doing there? I was worried about the police finding out that I'd planted the stuff on Sapphire. I couldn't tell."

"Do you have a name for this guy?"

"No. He's thirty-something. He works for the band, I think."

"And you'd definitely recognize him?"

"Yes."

The detective sighed. "All right, Lianne. We may have to organize a line-up. Wait here, please."

The band sat with their manager and security chief. If either of the two older men had recognized Stephanie, neither of them had indicated it. Both were preoccupied. Stephanie sat with her head on Fox's shoulder. They were all waiting to be told that they could go.

A detective came in and spoke to Jim and Hud. "I wonder if you two gentlemen would mind helping us? We've got an identity parade on and we're short of a couple of men, medium height, in their mid-thirties. It'll only take five minutes. Would you mind?"

The two men looked at each other quizzically, as if both were trying to come up with a reason to refuse. If so, they couldn't think of one. Once they'd left the room, the detective turned to the band. "You can go home now. Make sure we know how to reach you."

They said their goodbyes outside the station. Chris and Kerri went back to their flat. Stephanie went with Fox to his hotel room. They agreed to meet the lawyers, as planned, the next day. It didn't matter that Trudi was dead. They'd all had enough. The sooner that Face To Face was disbanded, the better.

When they got back to the hotel, Fox switched his mobile phone back on. He was in the shower when the thing rang. Steph brought it to him.

"Hunter."

Wrapped in a towel, Fox thanked the detective for finding Sapphire.

"So I guess this is goodbye," Fox said. "There'll be a bonus for you."

"You've paid me enough already," Hunter said, "but I've got a bonus for you. Some information I picked up while I was tracking down your friend."

Fox asked what it was. Hunter told him. Fox was stunned. He thanked Hunter, then joined Steph in the bedroom.

"What is it?" she asked. "You look like you've seen a ghost."

"It's more than that," Fox said. "I've seen *through* a ghost: Trudi Garth."

He told her what Hunter had told him.

"That explains a lot," Sapphire said when he'd finished, "but it still leaves the question: who killed her, and why?"

Fox picked up the phone again.

"Who are you calling?"

"The police. Find out if they've made an arrest."

He got through to the detective in charge. She was giving nothing away. Fox shook his head to tell Steph that they hadn't made an arrest.

"Listen," he told the detective inspector, "I've got some information you might be able to use. I think we ought to set a trap…"

37

"I'd like to postpone this meeting," Hud said the next morning, in a smart solicitors' conference room. "Jim and I have been up half the night, trying to help the police work out who killed Trudi."

"And did you succeed?" Fox asked.

Hud shook his head.

"I'm off to get some kip," Jim said.

"Would you mind staying a while?" Kerri said to him. "We might need your advice."

Jim looked confused but flattered. "About what?" he asked.

"It's kind of … sensitive. Tell me, Hud, who do you think killed Trudi?"

"Two options," Hud said. "Either it was a freak thing, an accident, or this crazy girl did it. She'd already stabbed Trudi once, left a nasty scar. Trudi kept it quiet because she didn't want the publicity and the girl was mentally ill. If only she'd pressed charges…"

"All right," Fox said. "Let's get this over with. There're a few things we need to go over, on the record. Everyone agrees to this being tape-recorded?"

Nobody objected. The solicitor switched a tape recorder on. Hud's lawyer switched his on, too.

"Before we discuss what happens to Face To Face," Fox said, "there are a couple of things we need to clarify. Hud, last night, in front of witnesses, Trudi said that you knew about Art's heart condition, that you planned for him to die and were counting on the publicity."

He was stretching what she'd said a bit, but Hud obviously believed him.

"Trudi said *that*? She must have been angry about something. It's rubbish. Trudi had quite an imagination."

Fox nodded. He'd never expected Hud to confess to that one. With Trudi dead, it was impossible to prove. "And then there was Sapphire leaving the band," he said. "She quit of her own accord, I gather."

"I told you all about it at the time."

"She wasn't pushed, to make way for Trudi Garth, for instance?"

"No," Hud said. "Of course not."

"You're lying."

The office door opened and Steph walked in. She'd spent the morning shopping, and having a wig made. Now she looked like her old self, only older, and more confident. "Tell the truth, Hud," she said.

Hud rolled his eyes, then stuttered out the story that the rest of them knew already: Sapphire lying about her age, her background.

"But that's not all of it, is it?" Fox asked, when he'd finished.

"I don't know what you mean."

"You'd never have thrown Stephanie out unless you had a replacement ready."

"I don't—" Hud began, tiredly, but Fox didn't let him finish.

"In fact, there was no real reason to get rid of her, was there? Work permits could have been sorted out. The publicity about her only being seventeen wouldn't have hurt. Except for one thing…"

"What?"

"Your girlfriend."

"I don't have a girlfriend," Hud said. "Look, what is this?"

Stephanie slid a photo across the table. "Are you sure?"

Hud picked it up. "This was fifteen years ago."

"But it's you, isn't it?" Stephanie said. "The Tempest Twins featuring Jeremy Hutchinson, now known as "Hud" Hutchinson and Sandra Garth, now known as the late Trudi Garth."

"Yes," Hud said. "Trudi and I go back a long way."

"Why didn't you tell us?" Chris asked.

"You were rivals. Anyway, I mentioned that I nearly managed The Ghosts."

"Yes," Fox said. "So you did. In fact, you set the group up, didn't you? Just like you did Face To Face."

"I…" Hud didn't finish the answer.

"I spoke to Tina Toldeo this morning," Fox said. "She confirmed that. You were still Trudi's boy-friend then, weren't you?"

"For a while."

"Only Trudi liked the high life and she dumped you."

"Yes," Hud admitted. "She did."

"Which was when you decided to set up another group who'd be even bigger than The Ghosts. You didn't make the same mistakes. This time, you had the contracts drawn up to give you total control…"

Hud sighed. "All this is true, but so what? It's water under the bridge. It won't bring Trudi back, or help us to work out whether Face To Face have a future."

"Let me take over the story," Kerri said. "You see, I've been trying to work something out. That night, at the hotel, when Alan Mackay took our photo-graphs, I wasn't the only person whose picture he took coming out of a room where they shouldn't have been."

"What do you mean?" Hud asked, but Kerri didn't answer.

She turned to Jim. "You know what was in the photographs, don't you? Hud sent you to negotiate with Mackay. You must have known."

"So?" Jim said. He was beginning to look worried, too.

"The thing is, when you – or somebody – went to see him, Alan Mackay wasn't alone."

Jim glanced at Hud for confirmation and Fox knew that they'd got him.

"There was a witness," Kerri said. "She knows what was in the photographs, why Hud had to have them destroyed. It wasn't big news that Chris and I were sleeping together. There'd already been speculation in the press about that. No, the big news was that Trudi Garth was sleeping with the band's manager."

Jim was silent. Hud was beginning to look angry. Stephanie spoke.

"How often did she sneak in to see you, Hud? We know that she was visiting you at the hotel in Birmingham when Lianne Hobbs stabbed Trudi. Is that why she didn't press charges, because she didn't want the media to find out that she was sneaking around hotel rooms, seeing a rival group's manager? You must have been so relieved when I gave you an excuse to get rid of me. What would you have done otherwise – had me killed, like Alan Mackay?"

Hud put his head in his hands. Stephanie turned to Jim.

"However much he's paying you, it can't be enough. The police have a witness who saw Hud meeting Alan Mackay, then driving him off to his death. She saw Hud climbing up the lighting rig, when you say that he was with you all the time. The only thing they hadn't put together was Trudi being Hud's girlfriend."

Hud got up. "I don't have to listen to any more of this."

"I'm afraid you do," the solicitor said, speaking for the first time. "You can speak here, or I can arrest you on suspicion of two murders."

"We forgot to mention," Fox said. "Ms Prescott's got a law degree, but she's also an inspector in Westminster CID."

Hud sat back down again.

"Why did you do it?" Chris asked.

Hud looked at Jim. The security chief shook his head. He wasn't going to protect the manager any more.

"I was in love with her," Hud told them.

"We'll need a little more than that," DI Prescott said.

212

38

"At first it was brilliant," Hud told them. "We were young, The Tempest Twins were going to be huge, we thought. But it didn't work out. The group died a death and Trudi left me. She went into heavy metal. I formed Famous with a couple of mates and we did OK: two top-twenty hits. But I worked out that I didn't have enough of what it takes to make it to the top. So I went into management.

"Once I'd become a success, Trudi got back in touch. I was still hurt over how she'd treated me, but I was a sucker for her. We became lovers again. I built The Ghosts for her, like Fox said. But as soon as the band were successful, they dumped me. Trudi tried to blame it on Tina, but I knew what she was about by then. Trudi wanted to be with rich, good-looking rock stars, not a boring, balding manager. She left me behind.

"So I set up Face To Face. This time, I kept complete control, or so I thought. I didn't know about Art's heart condition. That was really a shock. I'd never have let him join if I'd known, for both of our sakes." He looked at Stephanie, who had now taken off her wig. "I didn't know about Sapphire being under age, either. I suspected that there was something dodgy about you, but you had so much raw talent that I took the risk.

"The only uncomfortable thing about doing Face To Face was that it brought me into contact with Trudi again. I still felt the same. And she started being nice to me. She was unhappy in The Ghosts. She and Tina kept falling out, mainly because Tina was more talented than her and wanted to call the shots. Also, the group weren't as successful as she'd hoped. Our original strategy was that The Ghosts would crack America, then Trudi would go solo, become some kind of superstar. Without me there to guide them, it didn't happen.

"Even so, I was as surprised as anybody else when Trudi quit The Ghosts. It was a big risk. For a couple of months, I didn't see her. She'd been feeling around for a solo deal, but nobody was willing to pay the kind of money she thought she was worth. So she turned up at my place and, fool that I am, I took her back. It was going to be different this time, she said. We'd get married, have babies. She'd had enough of being a rock star.

"But she was lying. When Alan Mackay caught

us leaving that bedroom together, Trudi went ape. I argued that the photos weren't all that important. They'd just be a little embarrassing. Trudi wouldn't have it. She had to get rid of them, and him. So I arranged to meet Mackay, pretended I had the money. He got in the car. Trudi hit him from behind with a lead cosh she always carried with her for protection. We put him in the pool then she drove off. Only Jim knew that she'd been there. He lied about meeting Mackay so that the finger didn't point at me.

"After that, we were very careful. I started to notice that Trudi had stopped talking about babies and started talking about music again. Then she got stabbed and I had to look after her. She was so grateful. I thought that we'd finally got it together. I proposed and she accepted. We had a wonderful time. But, as Trudi got better, she started talking about joining Face To Face.

"I thought she was mad. Trudi faked her age, but we'd known each other since secondary school. I knew she was nearly twice as old as the rest of the band. But she was insistent. I'd made Face To Face into the most successful group in the world, she said. I spent so much time with them we could be together more if she was in the group. We could be together all the time. When she put the idea like that, it made sense.

"But I resisted. Sapphire was the most popular member. It wouldn't be easy to get her out of the group. Trudi was still recovering from surgery. She wasn't well enough to play again. But then, at Christmas, Sapphire told me she'd lied about her age and other things." He turned to Stephanie. "I'm sorry. I should have protected you. But all I could think about was Trudi. Here was the perfect chance to get her into the group. So I took it."

He stopped.

"You still haven't explained what happened last night," Sapphire said.

"Can't you guess?"

"We'd like it in your own words," Inspector Prescott said.

"Just before she went on stage, Trudi told me that she was leaving. I never put her on a contract like the rest of the group. She was a free agent. You've heard of…" He named the boss of one of America's biggest record labels. "He'd offered her a solo deal. Twenty million for two albums, superb royalties. She was sleeping with him, of course. I could tell that by the way she talked about him. She was going to fly to LA today, just as soon as she got out of this meeting."

"So you killed her?" the inspector asked.

"I didn't mean to," Hud said. "I only wanted to hurt her. I didn't really know what I was doing. When she went back on stage to do that encore, something inside me snapped. I spotted that spare camera, mounted on the lighting rig, and I went for it. I wasn't worried about being caught. I didn't care about anything except Trudi.

"But I didn't mean to kill her. I thought the camera would knock her out – fracture her skull, maybe break a few ribs. Then she wouldn't be able to go to America. She'd have to stay here and let me look after her. That was what I liked best, you see, caring for Trudi. After the stabbing, those were the best times… Anyway, the camera missed her, but she took a step the wrong way, and the wire was so sharp…" He began to cry. "I don't know if I can live with what happened."

After a while Hud recovered himself and held out his hands. "You want to handcuff me?"

"I don't think that'll be necessary," the inspector said. "You'd better accompany me to the station." She looked at Jim. "You'd better come, too. We'll have some charges for you."

She thanked the others. Now there was just the four of them and Hud's lawyer, who was phoning a criminal lawyer to represent the manager and security chief. When he'd finished his call, Chris, Kerri, Fox and Stephanie were still sitting in shocked silence.

"What's the position with the band?" Chris asked, as the lawyer prepared to leave.

The man thought for a moment. "Hud intended to persuade you to carry on. But that was before he confessed to mur—" he corrected himself. "Manslaughter and assisting a murder."

"What if we want to?" Fox asked. "I mean, continue."

Fox looked at Stephanie. Suddenly the thought of playing music with her again was the most appealing thing in the world. She nodded.

"He can't manage you from prison," the lawyer said. "No judge in the country would uphold your original contracts anyway – they're hugely restrictive."

"So we can carry on?" Chris said.

The lawyer smiled at Kerri, who grinned, then turned to Stephanie and Fox.

"You can carry on by all means. But there is a slight problem. Your manager undoubtedly owns the name of the group. His being in custody doesn't affect that. If you want to keep the name you'll have to pay him a substantial amount of money, and it may take a long time to settle."

"Who cares about the name?" Fox said.

"I always hated it anyway," Steph admitted.

There was a knock on the door. A tousle-haired youth put his head around it.

"Who are you?" the lawyer asked.

"My name's Jem," the youth said. "The police said that Face To Face were here. There's somebody needs a word with them."

"I'm done," the lawyer said, putting away his tape recorder and note pad. "I'll be in touch."

"I've persuaded them to see you," Jem said.

Lianne stepped into the room, light-headed from lack of sleep. The unreality of the situation hit her.

Here she was with four of the most famous people in the world. And, amazingly, *they knew who she was*.

"I just wanted to say hello," she said. "Hi."

Each of the group said "hello" or "hi" back. Lianne spoke to Sapphire. "I made some stupid phone calls and I put that cocaine in your purse. I'm sorry."

"It's OK," Sapphire said. "You spotted Hud last night. Without you as a witness, he might have got away with it. So thanks."

"It's really sad that you're splitting up," Lianne said. "I still think you're the best group in the world."

"Me, too," Jem said.

"Actually," Sapphire told her, "we might have changed our minds." She turned to the others. "What do you reckon? A couple of months to recover and write a few new songs? Then record a new album, pick a new name and get back on the road?"

"Sounds good to me," Fox said.

Chris and Kerri nodded enthusiastically. Lianne grinned.

"I'm so glad," she said. "Hey, I've just finished school. Any chance of a job in your fan club?"

"We'll see what we can do," Chris told her.

"Sure," Kerri said. "I'm starving. Would you guys like to come to lunch?"

"Try and stop us!" Jem said.

The six of them set off into the sunlit London street: three couples, hand in hand, smiling broadly. Lianne felt proud. Her life had come full circle:

she'd held on to her boyfriend, made up with Sapphire, and maybe even had a job.

It had all worked out. Everybody seemed so happy that Trudi Garth was dead. The event had brought Face To Face together again, made them into a proper group.

And it was all thanks to her. Not Hud. *Her.* For Lianne had had her own plan to kill Trudi Garth. Early the day before, she'd sneaked up the lighting rig and carefully attached razor sharp wire along the lead attached to the reserve camera. She'd planned to do what Hud did, only more efficiently. But when she went to do it, Hud was already there. She'd thought he'd caught her out. Instead, he'd carried out the plan for her.

Should Lianne tell the others what she'd done? They'd all wanted Trudi dead. They ought to be grateful. Lianne considered telling them then and there, as they all sat down in the smart restaurant and ordered champagne.

No, she thought. *Better to keep quiet.*

She didn't want them thinking she was crazy.